ONCE UPON

AMERICA

Blima Deutsch Silverman

ILLUSTRATIONS BY FAYGIE SILVERMAN

ONCE UPON AMERICA

Jewish stories
of
here and now

FELDHEIM
Jerusalem / New York

First published 1983
Hardcover edition: ISBN 0-87306-327-9
Paperback edition: ISBN 0-87306-335-x

Phototypeset at the Feldheim Press

Philipp Feldheim Inc.
96 East Broadway
New York, NY 10002

Feldheim Publishers Ltd
POB 6525 / Jerusalem, Israel

Printed in Israel

✳ *To my parents*

Mr. and Mrs. I. Deutsch

whose rich stories

of our European heritage

have always been a source of inspiration to me.

And with warmest thanks

to my husband and children

for their constant interest and encouragement.

Preface

A world ends, a world begins. But even beginnings must start somewhere.

The beginnings of European Jewry stretch far back into the annals of our history. For two thousand years, vital Jewish communities dotted the European continent. World War Two spelled the abrupt and tragic end of this remarkable Jewish world, but the seeds for a new beginning had already been planted on faraway shores.

Since its earliest history, small numbers of Jews had always lived in the United States. In the 1880s, however, mass migrations from Europe brought a large influx of Jewish immigrants to America, marking a major turning point for the fledgling Jewish community.

The arrival of scores of thousands of Jewish refugees after World War II marked another milestone, for now, in addition to large numbers of observant Jews, *roshei yeshiva* and Torah scholars also entered the American scene. Wherever they settled, they promptly set about organizing American yeshivos and day schools, thereby laying the foundation for the development of a vibrant new Orthodox community in the United States.

The stories in this book are a kaleidoscopic view of this new community. They deal with young people born and educated in America but nourished by the spiritual roots of their European ancestors. The first two stories, however, deal with the Old World. They are a recognition of indebtedness to those who, for two millennia, and despite great dangers and difficulties, lovingly and faithfully tended the Jewish garden and prepared the soil for the flowering of the Jewish New World.

contents

❋ A Kick in Time

❋ The birds twittered and chirped in the meadows, and the sun felt warm and good. Shragi was happy, very happy. He was home in Karlinovke, Russia, and it would soon be Pesach. He had done very well on his examinations at the yeshiva, and his father, Reb Mottel, was pleased with him. In fact, Reb Mottel was so pleased that he was allowing Shragi to go to Odessa for a few days with Uncle Shimon. Shimon was a cloth merchant, and he was going on a buying trip before the holiday.

As Shragi led his father's five new horses out to pasture, he sang out loud. And then, smiling to himself, he thought, "Here I am, eighteen years old and finally getting to go to Odessa." Shragi stroked the back of the black mare standing beside him. "You're a beauty of a horse," he murmured. "I'd love to ride you."

Shragi had always had a passion for horses. Living on a farm, he had learned to ride very early in life, and he took great pleasure in the swift and graceful movements of a horse running with the wind. Reb Mottel had a dairy farm with many horses, mainly for delivery purposes. These five new ones had just been broken in.

Shragi couldn't resist the urge to ride. He saddled the black mare and away they went, over the lush green grass that carpeted the meadow—faster and faster, until the wind took his breath away. He was feeling elated when suddenly, without warning, the horse reared. Whinnying loudly, she threw her mighty hoofs into the air. Shragi tried desperately to hold on but was thrown to the ground. He fell under the mare, and terror-stricken, he watched her hoofs hover in the air above his body. He tried to roll out of the way, but everything happened so fast that it was too late. The horse came down with a mighty blow on his left thigh. Pain wracked his body, and he fainted.

When he regained consciousness, his parents and three of his brothers were standing over him. His leg felt as though it were on fire. The throbbing was unbearable.

"Oy, yoi, yoi, *mein kind, mein kind,*" sobbed his mother.

His father and brothers put him onto a stretcher they had improvised and slowly, gently, carried him back to the house. Shragi's brother Yerachmiel hurried into town to call Dr. Kalefsky while the family tried to make Shragi as comfortable as possible. Soon, a small, heavy-set, bearded man with a homburg knocked at the door. Reb Mottel ran to answer it.

"Come in, Dr. Kalefsky, come quickly. He is in great pain."

Dr. Kalefsky adjusted his glasses, removed his coat and followed Reb Mottel into the back room.

The sun's rays lit up the spacious bedroom. Shragi lay on the bed, moaning. His mother stood beside him covering his head with a cool, wet cloth.

Dr. Kalefsky carefully removed the leg of Shragi's pants to examine the injury.

"Please, everyone out of the room," ordered the doctor. "I will take care of it. Out, out, right now! Yes, you too, Mother."

They all went into the big kitchen and sat at the long table—Reb Mottel, his wife Rachel, their six other sons and their only daughter, Chaya. It was quiet as they said *tehillim* and awaited the news of Shragi's condition. Reb Mottel lit a pipe and began to pace the floor, nervously pulling on his beard.

When the bedroom door opened, everyone jumped from their chairs.

"Is Shragi all right?"

"Can we see him now?"

"Let me go in."

"Shh," whispered the doctor. "I gave him a sedative. He is sleeping now. He needs his rest. He will need to wear a cast and stay off his feet for a good while, but I think Shragi will be good as new in a few weeks. That was a nasty accident and he is lucky to be alive."

Rachel lifted the corner of her apron and wiped the tears away. She hurried to put some money into the *pushke*.

That, of course, was the end of Shragi's trip to Odessa. He was very disappointed. Uncle Shimon said maybe next time, but next time would be during the winter session in the yeshiva and Shragi knew he couldn't go then.

Pesach came and went, and every day Shragi felt a little better. Finally, the day arrived when the cast was to be removed. Reb Mottel hitched the horses to the wagon, and he, Shragi and Yerachmiel rode into town.

The trip was only about five miles and the day was bright and clear. Shragi was pleased to be out again. The townspeople all came out to greet him, for Shragi was a favorite with everyone. He was cheerful, smiling, and affectionate, always ready to lend a helping hand or to do a favor. Everyone had come to visit when he was sick, not only to perform the *mitzva* of visiting the sick, but because they really liked him. And it was no wonder that they were so glad to see him up and about.

Shragi entered Dr. Kalefsky's office. Soon the cast was off, but much to everyone's dismay, an ugly, swollen purple scar marked his left thigh.

The doctor examined it carefully and announced that although the bone had healed, the wound had left this unsightly mark. He assured them that Shragi was perfectly fit and that he could do anything he desired. If the scar tissue bothered him, he could possibly have it removed. With a feeling of relief, the members of the family left Dr. Kalefsky's office.

As the weeks passed, Shragi made the decision to leave the scar alone. It did not bother him, and he decided not to bother it.

Summer became fall. The leaves on the trees turned orange, yellow and brown. The crisp autumn air brought color to the cheeks, and Sukkos was just around the corner.

"Here, Tatte, let me hold this side of the *sukka*. It's too heavy for you," said Shragi.

"Can I hang up the fruit yet?" asked Chaya.

"Not yet. You are too anxious, Chayale. We have to attach this last side and then put on the *sechach*," said Reb Mottel. "Meanwhile, help Mama with whatever she needs."

As the family worked with joy, preparing for the oncoming festival, a uniformed rider rode up to their home. After dismounting, he strode up the steps and knocked sharply on the front door.

Mama opened the door and gasped. It was a soldier!

There was nothing Russian Jews feared more than the Czar's army. The army took away young Jewish boys who were often never seen again. Once in the army, Jews could get no kosher food, nor could they keep any of the commandments. And they received the hardest work in the worst conditions. They were assigned night watch in the coldest weather, were among the first soldiers sent to the front, and in general were treated miserably. They were lucky to get home twenty years later in one piece.

Mama stared wide-eyed at the soldier. Her knees trembled.

"Who's there?" called Chaya as she came in from the kitchen. "Oh . . . Oh!" She stumbled over her feet, running as fast as she could to get her father.

"Tatte, oh, Tatte . . . a soldier . . . a soldier at our front door . . ."

Reb Mottel dropped his tools and rushed to the house. He was in time to hear the soldier announce that Shragi was to be drafted into the Czar's army. He was to appear for his physical examination the following Saturday morning punctually at ten o'clock. He could bring his own physician. With that, he clicked his heels and left.

Everyone was stunned. Mama wept as she clung to her young son.

Reb Mottel sent Yerachmiel into town immediately to inform the *rav*. That evening the entire Jewish community had a meeting. Rav Eliyahu Shefsky sat gravely at the head of the table. This was not the first time the community had been faced with such a situation, but each time the tragedy struck them anew.

Rav Shefsky began to speak. "My dear friends, I am sorry to inform you that this time our plight is much graver than usual. The old army doctor, Major Korda, has been relieved of his duty here. I was informed of this only yesterday." A shocked murmur went through the crowd.

"I doubt," continued the rabbi, "that we will be able to bribe the new doctor to say that our boys are unfit for service, as we did in the past with Major Korda, but we will make the collection as usual and we will use it as a last resort.

"Dr. Kalefsky, can you think of some way to convince the new doctor that Shragi has some physical problem?"

"Sometimes the drinking of large quantities of vinegar can cause a disturbance in the heartbeat," said the doctor. "We did this some years ago with the Shenker boy and it worked. It's worth trying."

"Very well," said Rav Shefsky, "and we will also proclaim a fast day tomorrow. *Tehillim* will be said around the clock. Beryl Pfeffer will collect funds. Everyone please contribute as much as you can. May *Hashem* in His great mercy grant us all freedom from the oppressors. Now let us all go home and finish our preparations for the *yom tov.*"

As the crowd left the room, they dropped coin after coin into Beryl's open bag, each person giving Shragi a *bracha* and praying that he be saved from the Czar's army.

Shabbos morning, the family walked gravely into town. Shragi had drunk large amounts of vinegar, but to no effect. Word had gotten around that the new doctor was a terror, plunging them into deeper despair.

After an early *minyan*, all the townsfolk came out to escort them. They waited as Shragi went into the building with his father.

Shragi was sent in alone to see the doctor. A few minutes later, Dr. Kalefsky was also called in, and the doors closed. The Jews of Karlinovke waited anxiously, like one, close family. Were not *kol Yisrael areivim zeh lazeh?* Each Jew was responsible for his fellow Jew!

The new doctor asked Shragi to undress and then began his examination. Every so often he made grunting noises to himself, but he said nothing to either Shragi or Dr. Kalefsky. Every few moments he marked the chart before him — heart, fine; lungs, fine; vision, fine; hearing, fine; blood pressure, fine.

In the last stages of the examination, he looked Shragi up and down and said suddenly, "What is this?" as he saw the large purple discoloration on Shragi's leg.

"What is that?" thought Dr. Kalefsky. "What is that? Why, that is a *nes* — a miracle sent by *Hashem* to keep Shragi out of the Russian army! And to think that in all the excitement I had forgotten about it!"

In his most professional manner, Dr. Kalefsky said, "It is a growth. I have been watching it for close to seven months now."

The two doctors began to speak in complicated medical terms. Shragi listened intently to the conversation. He could not understand what they were saying, but he began to have a glimmer of hope.

The army doctor examined the mark carefully. Again he conferred with Dr. Kalefsky.

Dr. Kalefsky argued vehemently on his patient's behalf, but the army doctor seemed determined to declare Shragi healthy. Shragi began to lose hope, but Dr. Kalefsky did not give up. He spoke again, using complex terms.

The army doctor examined the leg a third time. For the third time, Dr. Kalefsky contradicted the doctor's opinion.

Shragi was sent into the waiting room. He was very nervous. He took his handkerchief from his pocket and wiped his forehead. A large clock on the wall showed 12 o'clock noon. He had been there almost two hours.

Finally the door opened and the two men walked out. "You," grunted the army doctor, "can go back to your farm. The Czar's army does not need sick Jews."

Shragi could barely believe his ears. He wanted to leap for joy, to shout his happiness! Instead, he shakily took Dr. Kalefsky's arm. Together, they came out of the building to the still-waiting crowd.

No one spoke as they returned to the *shul*, but when they entered the building, Shragi shouted, *"Baruch Hashem,* I did *not* pass! I can stay home! *Baruch Hashem!"*

They cried and laughed and sang, praising *Hashem* for His great kindness. Then they made *kiddush* amidst much celebrating.

Shragi stood between his parents and looked into his father's eyes. "Tatte," he said, "it was truly *hashgacha pratis* — individual attention from *Hashem* — which caused me to get kicked by that mare. It was to spare me from a more horrible fate — the Czar's army."

"Yes, my son. Praised be *Hashem*. Often, things which seem so terrible to us turn out to be for the best."

Mama clung to the arm of her youngest son as they started the walk back home to enjoy this beautiful Shabbos day.

✳ *Night Riders*

✳ "Looks like it's going to snow," said Yankel to his father one *erev Shabbos*. "It'll probably be soon, too, maybe tonight or tomorrow."

"Then tomorrow night after *havdala*, you will have to load up quickly and go. But now, come. Let's get ready for Shabbos."

"Go! Again go!" thought Herschel to himself. "Where do they *go* all the time and what do they load into the wagon? Every time I come by, they stop talking. Nobody tells me anything. I'm just a baby around here."

Herschel's home was in Czechoslovakia, just outside Prague, and *erev Shabbos* was a busy, exciting time. With twelve children in the family and guests every week, there was always plenty to do. Everyone helped, even Herschel, who was second to the youngest. Although the well-to-do family could certainly afford hired help, they felt that there was special beauty in performing the *mitzvos* for Shabbos by themselves.

The fragrant aromas of gefilte fish and baking *challa* filled the oversized kitchen. Herschel dipped his finger into the raw potato *kugel* and received an affectionate slap on the hand from his sister Chasi, who put the pan into the stove.

"Hurry, Herschel, and put out Tatte's clean clothes for Shabbos, and this week make sure you polish his shoes!" With that, Herschel was lovingly shoved out of the busy kitchen.

As he shined his father's shoes, his mind turned again to the mysterious doings of his three older brothers. Where did they go in the middle of the night? What was in all of the boxes they loaded on the wagon? Why wouldn't they tell him about it? Maybe he would just find out all by himself! The more he thought, the angrier he became, and the angrier he became, the harder he rubbed. His father's shoes had never had a better shine.

Shabbos was always beautiful in Herschel's home. The table glowed with the Shabbos lights as Mama lit a candle for each child and one for Tatte and one for herself in the ornate silver candelabra. The family worked the fields on their large farm and managed a butter, eggs and cheese business. At week's end, although everyone was physically tired, the Shabbos brought them renewed strength which was felt by everyone in the house. If anyone happened to close his eyes or look sleepy at the table, Tatte would call,

"David, Aaron, sing a *nigun*," and the lively song would banish all weariness.

Tonight there were more guests than usual — travelers passing through and some boys on their way back to their yeshiva. It was a cheerful, noisy, happy group, except for Herschel who sat sulking at the end of the table. He was determined to find out what was going on. That night he lay awake under his heavy feather quilt and began to devise a plan.

There were many guests in the house, and most of them would be leaving at about the same time. While his family was busy with the good-byes, maybe Herschel could sneak away and hide under the tailgate of the wagon. If he wrapped himself up in the extra brown blanket they kept there, no one would notice him. He smiled to himself as he thought, "Good idea, Herschel!" He would say good-night and then go out the back door as everyone left through the front. In the dark, no one would see him running to the stable. Satisfied with his plan, he tucked himself deeper under the quilt and quickly fell asleep.

As soon as Shabbos was over, Yankel, David and Shalom hurried to load heavy boxes onto the wagon. Snow was falling and they wanted to be home by daybreak, if not earlier.

"Get some rope and tie the last few in," said Yankel.

"Never mind, it's late; just lift up the tailgate and latch it in place. It'll hold up. Let's get going," answered Shalom.

Herschel whispered a silent prayer that they wouldn't notice him. His scarf, however, was caught in the hook of the latch. As they lifted the tailgate of the wagon, there was a long ripping sound. Herschel clenched his teeth in fear, but in their eagerness to leave, no one heard the noise.

The brothers climbed into the front seat. David took the reins while Yankel and Shalom arranged the blankets over the boxes. Soon they were on their way.

The wind started blowing fiercely, scattering snow-flakes through the cold night air. Herschel was very uncomfortable in his position under the wagon. The force of the wind pushed and shoved him. They were traveling as quickly as the horses could go, and Herschel thought about climbing onto the top of the wagon and under the covers of the boxes.

They were nearing the edge of the woods now, and the brothers stopped to light their kerosene lamp. No one liked traveling through the forest at night. Too many things could happen.

"Let's go around the forest," said Shalom. "The snow is falling fast, and I don't want to get stuck in the woods. It's too dangerous."

"It's too long that way," replied Yankel. "We'll go straight through like we always do. Just light the lamp so we can get on with it. Hurry, I'm freezing."

"He's freezing!" thought Herschel. "What should I say? I can barely feel my feet. I'm beginning to think this wasn't such a good idea after all, and I don't want to go through the forest. I don't even like to go there in daylight." Herschel was sorely tempted to come out of his hiding place.

"Listen," said Shalom, "why don't we take the short-cut over the bridge? It's really the fastest way."

The brothers argued back and forth for a few minutes and finally decided that Shalom's idea was the best. Although it meant traveling through the woods for a short while, the bridge would shorten the distance considerably, providing it hadn't iced up. They would take the chance.

As the wagon lurched forward, the soft glow of the lamp brightened their spirits. Herschel cautiously lifted himself up from under the wagon, and peering over the rim, he waited for the proper moment. Then he slid quietly over the edge into the wagon, and under the blankets.

As they traveled over the bumpy road, the brothers watched the snow. It was an eerie scene, the onset of a blizzard. The wind howled through bent-over trees as the brothers urged the horses on.

Under the cover, Herschel stretched his hand out to the first box on his left and felt for an opening. He had to know what the boxes contained! The top was open, and he carefully put his hand inside. What he felt was soft and powdery and it filled the whole box. He took some out, but it was too dark to take a good look. Herschel slipped his fingers over to the next box and gently lifted the lid. It felt like cloth, different pieces. "Why, it's clothes," he thought. Clothes? Powder? What could these possibly mean? He tried to grasp a third box, but it was too far to reach without drawing attention to himself.

Suddenly the wagon slid across the road. Ice!

"Can we make it over the bridge?" asked David worriedly.

"If we hurry, we can get over before it freezes too badly. On the way home, we'll take another route," replied Yankel.

The horses moved slowly until they reached a bridge which spanned the small river running through the woods. Beyond the bridge was a town and an inn. The horses cautiously clattered over the old wooden slats, causing a hollow echo in the black, lonely night.

They proceeded very, very slowly. Suddenly Herschel felt the wagon lurch to one side and then swing over sharply to the other. The air was filled with the sound of fearful neighing.

"Hold the reins," Shalom yelled in panic. As the wagon slid backwards down the bridge, the latch shook loose and the tailgate fell open. Boxes began tumbling everywhere. Herschel suddenly found himself falling, slipping, sliding . . . and screaming.

He tried to grab something to hold onto, but he couldn't. Tumbling headlong out of the wagon, he rolled down across the bridge. He felt himself falling down, down, down into the freezing water below!

"Whoa, whoa, easy boy, steady there!" coaxed Yankel, trying to calm the terrified horses. As Yankel grappled with the horses, Shalom and David darted toward the screams piercing the air from the river.

"Hold on down there, hold on! Don't panic," shouted Shalom.

They slid down the icy embankment, clutching the oil lamp in an effort to see.

"There, over there! I see him! Here, David, hold the light — I'll get him!"

Shalom pulled off his heavy boots and overcoat, and plunged into the freezing waters.

"He's coming, he's coming," shouted David. "Try to stay afloat."

Shalom reached the thrashing, frantic figure. He managed to grab hold of a coat, but he was momentarily forced under by the heavy current. He surfaced and grabbed Herschel's arm, but the panicking Herschel pulled them both under the water again. Shalom was afraid they would both drown. He struggled to reach Herschel once more, this time stunning the youngster with a blow on the jaw. Fighting the current furiously, he managed to pull the half-drowned figure ashore.

Then, by the light of the oil lamp, the three brothers saw a shocking sight.

"Oh, no!"

"It's Herschel!"

"Are you all right?"

"What are you doing here?"

Trembling with cold and his face streaming with tears, Herschel revealed what he had done and why.

The brothers were at a loss as to what to do. On the one hand, there were two soaking-wet, chilled-to-the-bone people, liable to catch pneumonia. On the other hand, they were more than half-way to an important rendezvous. Finally, Yankel wrapped his youngest brother up in the brown woolen blanket, and put another blanket over Shalom, while David hurriedly reloaded the wagon. Yankel took hold of the reins and gently urged the horses to follow him over the bridge. They would try to reach the inn.

The warm glow of light from the inn looked inviting. Although time was of the essence, the brothers had no choice but to stop. Shalom and Herschel were left at the inn to dry their clothing and drink some hot tea. The proprietor was familiar with the brothers' nightly journeys, and he was their comrade in secrecy. All through the years he had never revealed what Yankel, Shalom and David were doing. Yankel and David left the inn, saying they hoped to return in two hours.

They resumed their journey but soon stopped at the Levy household.

"Quickly now! The box with the clothes. No, not that one—the one with the baby clothes. Good, now the carrots and potatoes. Don't forget the milk. Those babies need milk. A little more. Quietly. Let's not wake them."

"All right. Let's move on."

Next they stopped at the Kepfers. Here they left coats, a large box of firewood and a carton of flour. The Kepfers were elderly people who needed extra fuel to keep warm.

Then they went to the Schwartzes, leaving meat and a case of eggs which, miraculously, had not fallen out of the wagon. Although some were broken, most were intact.

"Look at these eggs," remarked David, lifting the case from the wagon. "*Hashem* certainly watches over things we need in order to perform a *mitzva!*" Mrs.

29]

Schwartz had been sick and needed good food to build up her strength. And so the brothers continued on in the dark of the night until their wagon was empty.

Back at the inn, Herschel demanded to know what was going on. Finally, Shalom explained, but not before making Herschel promise to keep their secret.

"You see, Herschel, there are many families in our town and the surrounding villages that are not as fortunate as we are. They work hard and try to manage, but sometimes things are very difficult for them. They don't always have enough food or clothing, and in the winter they don't have enough fuel to keep them warm. So Tatte and Mama fill up boxes of things for them— produce from the farm and old clothes—which we deliver."

"But why go at night? Why can't you give it to them during the day, when you can see where you're going?"

"Because then, my little brother, these people would be embarrassed and wouldn't want to take the things. No one feels good about accepting charity. The best way to help is to give so that the needy don't know who the giver is. We leave our boxes on their doorsteps at night, and when they find them in the morning, they needn't be embarrassed to take them."

"So why couldn't you tell me what you were doing?"

"Because, little one, we thought you might accidentally let it be known that we are the ones who leave these boxes in town, and that would have spoiled everything!"

"Do you really think I'm such a baby? I won't tell, but I also want to help share these *mitzvos*."

"I'm sure you do, but you're too young to go riding through the woods with us at night. You see what happened tonight with the snow and the ice. And, as I told you, this isn't the only town we go to. Sometimes we go to two or three towns that are nearby when we hear about people who need help."

"But I *want* to help! I'm big enough to do *something*."

"I suppose you are at that," said Shalom. "Well, we'll see."

David and Yankel soon returned, and the brothers started on their way home. During the trip, they all agreed that Herschel was still too young to accompany them on their trips, but since his desire to share in the *mitzva* was so great, he could help pack the boxes and load the wagon.

Herschel was satisfied with this promise, and he smiled happily at the thought of participating in such a great *gemilas chesed*. Feeling thoroughly content, he snuggled up against the strong, warm arm of his big brother, Shalom, and fell asleep.

❄ *Wet Shoes*

❄ Sara Lea forced back the heavy bolt and lifted the shade from the front door of the grocery. She rubbed her hand across the steam-coated glass and peered out into the early morning street.

It was cold and dark outside. The street lights were still lit, and she watched the heavy snowflakes tumble slowly earthward. Everything was very white and very beautiful, but she was glad to be inside — warm and safe.

Sara Lea turned on the light in the grocery so people would know it was open, and then she walked back to the apartment behind the store. There were two rooms behind the store, a kitchen and a bedroom. Sara Lea's parents had the bedroom, while she slept on a long couch in the kitchen.

She covered the couch and finished dressing by the warmth of the stove. The clock on the wall said six o'clock, and soon her father would begin to *daven*. Sara

Lea measured the coffee into the pot and set it on the stove.

She would have to stay home from school today because her mother was sick and could not tend the store. The little store didn't bring in enough money for all their needs, so for the past six years, since the depression of 1929, her father had a job in Uncle Yossi's business.

There was a tap at the door.

"Surunu, are you up yet?"

"Yes, Tatte."

"Did you turn on the light in the store?"

"Yes."

"Good."

Sara Lea's father, a heavy-set, bearded man, came into the kitchen and took out the bag which held his *tallis*.

"The coffee smells good," he told his daughter. "Mama is feeling a little bit better, but don't wake her up. She needs the rest."

Just then the tinkle of the bell on the front door let them know they had an early customer, and Sara Lea went quickly into the store.

"Good morning, Mrs. Snyder, what can I get you?"

"A dozen eggs, I want, please, and some sugar for coffee."

As Sara went to get the items, she watched Mrs. Snyder begin to open the bottles of milk and smell them. Her mother had told Mrs. Snyder not to do that at least a hundred times — it wasn't fair to the other customers — but she kept doing it anyway. Being alone in the store with her, Sara was tempted to say something, but she bit her tongue. She knew they couldn't afford to lose a customer. All they had was the very early or the very late trade, because most people preferred to shop at the new A & P which had opened up around the corner.

"Anything else, Mrs. Snyder?" she asked, forcing a smile.

"No, that's all. How much do I owe you?"

"Fifty-two cents."

"Put it on the bill, please."

"Again on the bill!" thought Sara Lea. "Don't people ever realize that we have to pay for things?" But she took out the pad and recorded the items, giving a copy to Mrs. Snyder.

Sara Lea hurried into the kitchen, washed and grabbed a bagel. She would have to eat something in a hurry because soon their suppliers would be making deliveries and then she wouldn't have time for breakfast. She set a place for her father and one for herself and took his lunch-pail out of the ice-box.

Sara Lea's father finished *davening,* ate quickly and hurried off to work, leaving his thirteen-year-old daughter alone with the store and her thoughts.

A few customers came and went, but they left very little in the cash register. The milkman, the breadman, and the cookie-man came with fresh supplies, and then it was quiet.

Sara Lea hoped her mother would get up before the schoolchildren came in for candy at lunchtime. When she was alone with them, they were very wild, and if they broke or destroyed things, it meant a loss of money which they couldn't afford.

Sara Lea sat behind the counter in the store, staring at the long icicles hanging from the awning over the front window. She noticed a man walking back and forth under the awning, blowing his hands to keep them warm. He wore a hat with a hole on one side, and his brown coat was shabby and worn. He had no boots, even though there was snow everywhere. Sara Lea thought how wet his feet must be. Soon he walked on, and she forgot about him.

A while later, the man returned, looking in the grocery window and pacing back and forth again. He kept putting his hand up to his moustache, nervously rubbing it back and forth. He looked so tired and pale. Sara Lea began to wonder about him. He shook his head, and again left.

Mrs. Kimmelman came in for two cans of tomato soup and a bottle of milk, and Sara Lea realized it was already eleven o'clock. Her mother was still not up. In less than an hour the children would be out of school for lunch.

About fifteen minutes later, the man in the brown coat was back under the awning, tugging at his moustache and staring into the window again. This time he timidly entered the grocery, rubbing his cold hands together.

"Can I help you?" asked Sara Lea.

"Well, you see—you—ah—you're here by yourself?"

"Is there something you'd like to buy?"

35]

"Your mama . . . can I talk to your mama?"

"She can't help you right now. Please, sir, is there something I can do for you?"

"Well, you see—I—uh—uh, I—lost mine job. I am hungry. You got lot of food in store. Please, little girl, to give me something to eat . . . please."

Sara Lea was stunned. She didn't know what to do. She didn't know if it would be all right to take something from the shelf, but her father had cautioned her not to wake her mother. Sara Lea thought a moment and then said, "Why don't you come back in a little while and then my mother will be able to help you."

The man gave a weary sigh, covered his face with his hand and turned his back to Sara Lea. He trudged wearily out into the cold, and she heard the snow crunching under his wet shoes as he went down the block. Sara Lea looked after him, filled with a mixture of compassion and guilt.

Half an hour later she heard the water running in the kitchen sink. She went in and found her mother.

"Good morning, Mama. Are you feeling better?"

"Oy, *mein kind*, a little better, *baruch Hashem*. I am so sorry you couldn't go to school today!"

"That's all right, Mama. I'm glad you're better."

"Was there any business?"

"Not too much, Mama. And Mrs. Snyder went and opened all the bottles again!"

"Nu, what can we do?"

"Mama . . ."

"Yes?"

"Mama, there was a man here today. He went back

and forth a couple of times and finally he came into the store."

"Yes . . . so?"

"He said he lost his job and was hungry and he wanted to know if I could give him something to eat."

"And you gave him, yes? Like a good girl?"

"No, Mama, I didn't know if I should and you were sleeping, so I told him to come back later."

"You didn't give him?"

"No, Mama."

"Oy! A person who tells you he is hungry comes into a store full of food and you tell him to come back later? No, my child, that is not right. Now, you will put on your hat and coat and boots, and you will go to look for him and bring him back."

"Mama, it's so cold outside!"

"All the more reason you should find him; not only is he hungry, he is cold also."

"But where should I look?"

"Up and down the streets until you find him."

Sara Lea went to the closet. She took out her heavy cardigan sweater, a scarf, her long blue coat and her rubber galoshes. She pulled a hat over her brown curly hair, and as she left the store, she tucked two candy bars deep into her coat pocket.

Where was she to look? She decided to walk two blocks in one direction, then turn right and walk two blocks in another. Pittsburgh is a hilly city, and this way, she decided, she wouldn't be climbing up and down quite as much. She was very systematic, starting her search on Bedford Avenue and walking all the way

to Dinwiddy Street. The man was nowhere in sight, and she was very cold and tired. She thought of going home, but she knew her mother would be disappointed if she returned alone. She stopped in a corner drugstore to warm up a little and thought about the man standing under their awning. How cold he must have been, and he had no galoshes, only wet shoes.

Munching on a candy bar, she left the drugstore and continued her search, remembering that the man was not only cold, but hungry. She was determined to find him.

She tried to imagine where a hungry person might go, and it occurred to her that he might try the *shul* on Webster Avenue. Mr. Weiss, the *shamash*, was usually there every afternoon, from before *mincha* until after *maariv*. She started to run, forgetting how tired she was, but when she reached the *shul*, the door was locked. Mr. Weiss hadn't arrived yet. Then where might the man in the brown coat be?

Sara Lea walked down the wide stairs leading from the *shul* to the street and sat down on the bottom step to think. Something on the far corner of the stairway caught her eye. It seemed to be a big bundle. She got up to investigate, and as she came nearer, she realized it was a person!

"Oh, my," thought Sara Lea, "it's that man! Is he dead? Did he freeze or die from hunger because I didn't give him anything to eat?"

Sara Lea stared at the pitiful form and then leaned over the man slightly. She heard his faint breathing. Relieved, she called, "Mister, mister, do you hear me? . . . mister, wake up . . . please wake up!" He didn't stir.

"What should I do?" she said aloud.

"Get up! Please get up . . . do you hear me, please . . . you have to get up. You must!" she called again.

Her voice became louder and louder until she realized she was screaming. As she turned to run for help, she thought she heard something. The man's eyes were open. He seemed to be trying to say something.

Sara Lea took the second chocolate bar from her pocket and gave the man a piece. As he chewed it, she kept talking and trying to reassure him. Then she went back onto the street to look for help, but it was so cold that very few people were out. She pulled off a low-hanging branch from the tree in front of the *shul* and brought it back for the man to support himself. When he finally managed to stand, she took off her scarf and gave it to him.

"Here," she said, "wrap this around your neck. I'm taking you home with me. It's not too far. You'll be able to make it all right."

Silently, the two figures made their way slowly through the alley behind the *shul*, and turned down the short-cut that led to the back of the store. The snow was getting thicker, and Sara Lea kept looking at his wet shoes.

Pushing open the back door, Sara Lea called, "Mama, Mama, I found him . . . Come quickly, Mama." The delicious warmth of the kitchen engulfed them, and the man sank wearily onto a chair.

Sara Lea's mother came in from the store followed by two customers, Mrs. Raymond and Mrs. Lieber, the doctor's wife. When they saw what condition the man was in, Mrs. Lieber left immediately to call her husband. Mrs. Raymond helped Sara Lea's mother wrap the man in blankets. Then they poured him a cup of hot coffee to help him warm up. As Sara Lea's mother placed food before him on the table, he told his story.

"Mine name is Beryl Kasselbaum. I am from de old country, Poland. I live mit mine cousin. But mine cousin lose all money and business. He become very, very sick, and . . . and . . . he die." Beryl wiped the tears from his eyes. "So now . . . I am by mineself." He paused as tears rolled down his cheeks.

"Oy," sighed Sara Lea's mother. "Nu, so what are you doing now?"

"I go from job to job. You see . . . I don't speak English good. I have no money, no house. Boarding house put me out."

"When," asked Sara Lea's mother, "did they put you out?"

"Two days."

"Oy! Two days in the snow and cold? *Nebach!*"

At that moment they heard the tinkle of the store bell, and Dr. Lieber came into the kitchen.

"Hello," said the doctor, "I hear you need help."

"Yes," said Sara Lea's mother. "This is Mr. Kasselbaum. Sara Lea found him in the snow."

"Hello, Mr. Kasselbaum, my name is Dr. Lieber. I'm going to check you over. Ladies, would you please leave the room."

41]

Turning to the patient, Dr. Lieber said softly, "Do you understand English?"

Beryl nodded.

"Good! Here, let's take your temperature," said the doctor as he shook down the thermometer and placed it in Beryl's mouth.

He took Beryl's pulse and listened to his heart and lungs.

"Breathe deeply, Mr. Kasselbaum . . . Let it out . . . Again, please."

Mr. Kasselbaum began to wheeze and cough.

"It's not as bad as it sounds," the doctor reassured the frightened patient. "Here are some pills; I want you to take two of them four times a day. Every time you eat and before you go to sleep. Do you understand?"

Beryl nodded.

"Now get plenty of rest and drink a lot of warm liquids."

"Liquid?" asked Beryl with a puzzled look on his face.

"Tea . . . hot tea."

"Yah. Thank you, Doctor, thank you."

As he entered the store, Dr. Lieber repeated the instructions to Sara Lea and her mother. "Don't worry. It's nothing serious. He'll be fine in a few days. Call me if you need me." With those words, he disappeared out the front door.

Sara Lea turned to her mother. "What will we do now, Mama?" she whispered in her mother's ear. "We can't send him away like this, can we? He doesn't have any place to go and he's sick."

"What will we do? We will keep Mr. Kasselbaum here in the store with us. We will keep him until he is well. Then your father will try to help him somehow. He will know what to do."

"Yes," thought Sara Lea, "Tatte will know what to do. He always does. He won't send someone like Mr. Kasselbaum away. And we'll have to see if we can find him a pair of galoshes."

❄ *Papa Krasner's Basement*

❄ Papa Krasner was getting on in years. You could
tell by the way his moustache drooped and his spectacles slid down his nose when he fell asleep on the
front porch rocker. If you caught him napping, he
would harumph, sputter and cough, and rattle his
newspaper. Then he would peek at you through the
corner of his eye to see if you had caught him, and he
would raise his eyebrows and harumph again.

You could also tell things weren't the same because
the boardinghouse didn't look the same as it used to
look. It needed painting and fixing. Mama Krasner
really kept the place going. Of course, she didn't cook
for the boarders anymore. Times had changed. It was
grand back in the "good old days" before World War II
when there were lots of nice, young Jewish boys to feed
and mother. But now, it was 1958 and the various
tenants who paid the rent complained that it was too
hot in the summer and too cold in the winter. In fact,
last winter the pot-bellied coal stove finally gave up,

and the Krasners' children — Miriam, Fayge, Moshe and Benny — called a company to install a new forced-air furnace. Papa Krasner protested violently, but to no avail. The last straw came when the workmen wanted to remove the old furnace from its place in the basement. Papa Krasner stationed himself in front of the pot-bellied stove, arms spread out to shield it, and refused to budge. If it went, he was going with it. They had to leave the old furnace in place and install the new one further away, with longer pipes to reach the ducts.

"Papa," argued Benny, "the new stove is better. It's more expensive."

"Ve don't need it," answered Papa. "Mine old stove is fine. Just needs a little fixin' up."

"Papa, it's so broken that the pipe over the furnace falls out if you slam the kitchen door upstairs. It could kill someone!"

"Ain't hurt no one yet."

The new heater went in but the old one stayed.

Mama tidied up as best she could, did the shopping and paid the bills. But it was getting hard for her. And with the neighborhood changing and the young rough-necks coming in, Mama thought very seriously about moving out. The children all wanted them to move, but Papa wouldn't hear of it.

"I got mine house, mine *shul* on de corner, and two blocks avay is de grocery, de drugstore and Sears. Vat more could I vant?"

This particular Tuesday afternoon, Papa was in his usual spot on the porch, watching the traffic on Fax-lawn Avenue. It was a sunny summer day in Memphis, and Papa clocked the transit bus with his pocket watch. It was right on schedule as it stopped across the street from his house. Much to his surprise, he saw a middle-aged, bearded man, dressed in a black suit and carrying a satchel, come walking up his driveway.

"Mr. Krasner?"

"Yes."

"*Shalom aleichem,*" said the bearded gentleman as he extended his hand.

"*Aleichem shalom,*" replied Papa Krasner.

"I'm Rabbi Saperstone. I was told that you have a room I might use while I make my collections here in town."

"Vell, vat do you know," Papa Krasner smiled happily, "a *meshulach!* Ve ain't had a *meshulach* stay mit us in years now dot everybody got fency and moved out from de neighborhood. Mama, Mama," he cried excitedly, "come here qvick. Ve got company."

Mama Krasner came running in from the kitchen, drying her hands on her apron as she appeared at the front door.

"Oh, my, my. It's been years since we used our '*meshulach* room' as we call it. Nobody wants to stay in this section anymore. Nice to have you. Come on in and have a cup of tea while I prepare linen for you. Oh, how nice, how nice . . ." said Mama as she hurried to put up the kettle.

While Rabbi Saperstone was sipping tea through little cubes of sugar, the Krasners received another visitor. Their daughter Miriam came excitedly through the front door.

"Mama, Papa . . . Where are you? I have great news!"

"We're in the kitchen, Miriam, with Rabbi Saperstone."

"Oh, hello, Rabbi Saperstone. Pleased to meet you. No, please don't get up. Finish your tea. Mama, Papa, could I see you in the front room a minute? Please excuse us, Rabbi Saperstone."

"Certainly."

They entered the living room and Miriam began, "I have the loveliest house for you. I just got a new listing this morning."

Mr. Krasner put up his hand in protest, but before he could say anything, Miriam continued.

"Papa, please, just listen. It's perfect! Five rooms — you could have an extra bedroom for as many *meshulachim* as you want! And a big fenced-in backyard with beautiful trees. And it has a porch, Papa — not in front, but in back — a beautiful screened-in back porch. When the *aineklach* come, you can sit on the porch and watch them play in the yard and not have to worry about the buses on Faxlawn Avenue. It's on Brentwood Lane, Papa, just two blocks from your *shul*. It's perfect — absolutely perfect!"

"You vant Mama and I should give up our income and our home?"

"But, Papa, you'll have a new home, near your children, in a safe neighborhood. And the best part is, you don't have to give up this house either. They only want four hundred dollars down, so you can buy it and keep this house to pay off the note. Can you believe it?

Look, I rushed over there first thing this morning. It's in great condition, and I want to write up a contract for you today before someone else is interested."

"You been writing up contracts for us since you got your real estate license last year, but I'm not movink!"

"Papa," said Mrs. Krasner, "maybe we should look. It don't hurt to look."

"What for to look? I ain't gonna buy!"

"Papa," said Miriam, "this neighborhood isn't safe anymore. You've got to move. At least *look* at it. You might like it. Think about it. Won't it be nice to be near all of us every Shabbos? And the children can see you more often, not just once or twice a week."

"That would be so nice, Papa," said Mama with a wistful look on her face. "Please, let's just look."

"I can't leave de house to look at notink til Tursday."

"Why not?"

Papa looked back and forth furtively, and whispered, "I got de *shul* treasury money in de basement."

"You've got what?" exclaimed Miriam, shock spread all over her face.

"Vell, de safe broke in *shul* and somebody got to keep de money, and I'm de treasurer. Nu, so I'm keeping it until Tursday ven dey fix de safe."

"Why didn't you put it in the bank?" ·

"Don't trust no banks. Never put a nickel in banks."

"But you can't leave the money in the basement," insisted Miriam. "It's too dangerous. Let's put it in the bank right now."

"NO! Dat's final. It stays here and I stay mit it."

"Papa, sometimes I don't understand you. It's . . ."

"You don't need to understand me — just listen to me. I'm your father, so just give me respect. De money stays mit me. Mama wants to look at the house, take her. I stay here mit Rabbi Saperstone."

And with that, Papa Krasner adjusted his spectacles, harumphed, and walked back into the kitchen.

"Mama, I'm calling Benny to come here right now and get that money."

"I been arguing with Papa since Sunday, but it don't do no good."

"Oy! It's been here since Sunday? How much is it, do you know?"

"Not exactly. A couple hundred dollars, I think."

"Where is it?"

"In the old stove."

"Mama, come on, get your purse. Let's go out to look at the house. We'll stop at Benny's office on the way and tell him."

"I can't go right now. I got a roast in the oven, and I have to cook a little something extra since Rabbi Saperstone is here."

"I'll tell you what. It's almost three-thirty already and I have to show a couple of houses this afternoon, so why don't you eat early and I'll pick you up right after supper, OK? We'll still have plenty of light to see everything. I just won't show this house to anyone else until tomorrow, so you'll get first chance."

"Fine," smiled Mrs. Krasner, clasping her hands together in anticipation.

Miriam stopped at Benny's office. Benny was the eldest son, and he had more influence on Papa than the others. He was out, however, so she left a message and returned home.

After dinner she drove back to her parents. Mama Krasner was waiting on the porch when Miriam arrived. She got into the car.

"Did Benny call, Mama?"

"No."

"I wonder if he got my message."

Miriam thought a moment, and then continued, "Is Rabbi Saperstone out collecting?"

"Not tonight. He is very tired. He traveled by bus all the way from Dallas and he's going to bed early. He'll start collecting tomorrow."

"Good. I hate to leave you two alone with all that money in the house. Mama, wait until you see this house!" said Miriam as she backed the car out of the driveway.

The brick, ranch-style home was set far back from the street. Magnolia trees graced the lush green front lawn. Green shutters matched the grass and gave the house a quaint, fairy-tale look. The living-dining room was large, and the kitchen was the *pièce de résistance*. Mama Krasner fingered the modern counter tops and oohed and ahed over the appliances.

"Where do I wash clothes? In the basement?"

"No basement, here, Mama."

"No basement? Then how . . ."

"Look," interrupted Miriam as she pushed back a folding door to the side of the kitchen, "a hidden laundry room. No more steps to climb all the time, Mama. It's right here, near the kitchen. Now, come to the back yard."

Mama Krasner couldn't believe her eyes. "It's like having your own park," she thought to herself, "trees and trees."

"Two apple trees and a peach tree and look, Mama . . ." called Miriam as she pointed to the far corner of the yard, "a grapevine with real concord grapes. Papa can make his own wine." Miriam went on and on, extolling the virtues of the house and the neighborhood.

Meanwhile Papa Krasner and Rabbi Saperstone settled down at the dining room table with two glasses of tea and two large *gemaras*.

"Ach, a pleasure to sit and learn. Ain't got nobody in the neighborhood to learn mit no more. My son Moshe comes every Tursday night, and de Rabbi gives a *shiur* on Shabbos, but it was nice when I could learn with someone every night. Times change."

"Maybe you should change with the times, Mr. Krasner. You certainly would have a more Jewish environment if you moved nearer your children."

"I'm too old to pick up and move."

"Never too old to be near Torah, Mr. Krasner. Nu, let's begin. I'm in *Berachos, daf beis, amud aleph. Me-eimosai* . . ."

Rabbi Saperstone swayed. "When can you begin to say the *Shema* at night . . ." he began chanting.

For over an hour they bent over their books, losing

track of time and surroundings. They were so engrossed that they failed to hear the footsteps on the walk, or to see a silent figure peering through the kitchen window. The tall, thin figure crept furtively from window to window, and satisfying himself that only the two men were in the house, he moved quietly to the rear of the house where he tested the back window and found it unlocked. He put on a pair of gloves, pulled a scarf over his face, lowered his cap over his eyes and slipped noiselessly through the kitchen window.

The two men in the dining room, absorbed in their learning, were totally unaware of his presence. The thief looked through a crack in the kitchen door. Papa Krasner's back was toward him. Good! He'd get hold of the old man first. After taking a gun from his pocket, he swung the kitchen door open in one swift motion and leaped upon Papa Krasner, holding him by the neck while pointing the gun straight at Rabbi Saperstone.

Papa Krasner gasped, his spectacles rolled down his nose and his moustache twitched. Rabbi Saperstone calmly raised his hands and his eyes toward Heaven. "*Ribono shel olam*, help!" he prayed silently.

"Don't move," grunted the thief.

"How ken I?" asked Papa Krasner. "If I move, I get choked! Ach! Let go—I ain't going noveres."

"Sit down and be quiet or I'll shoot," threatened the thief as he let go of Papa Krasner's neck.

"OK, old man," he said, pushing the gun against Papa Krasner's neck, "take this rope and tie your friend to his chair."

53]

"Vat for? He ain't going noveres neider. Vat you vant here? Ve ain't got notink."

"Oh, yeh, Krasner? We'll see. Now do as I say, or else!"

"Listen to him, please, Mr. Krasner," pleaded Rabbi Saperstone.

The thief pulled out a thick rope from his pocket and directed Papa Krasner to tie the rabbi up, his hands behind the chair.

"His legs, too," continued the thief.

Having accomplished that, he warned Rabbi Saperstone not to scream, because if he did he would shoot them both.

"Now, old man, where's the money you took home from the synagogue?"

"How you know bout dat?" asked Papa Krasner, adjusting his spectacles so that he could see the thief better.

"Never mind how I know. Just get it, or else!"

"Please, Mr. Krasner, don't argue with him," cautioned Rabbi Saperstone.

The thief shoved the gun at Papa Krasner's back, urging him on.

"Where'd you hide it?"

"OK, OK, I show you. Don't you know you shouldn't steal? It ain't right. Better to get a job. You strong and healty. Vork for a . . ."

"Don't give me no lectures, man. Quit stalling and get the money!"

The thief's tone of voice was getting angrier and angrier, and Papa Krasner decided to obey.

"It's in de basement."

"Awright, let's go then," he said, shoving the elderly man toward the basement door at the side of the kitchen.

When they were out of the room, Rabbi Saperstone searched frantically for a telephone. There was none in the dining room. He would somehow have to get into the kitchen and knock the receiver off the hook to get help. He began to hobble and jump together with the chair he was tied to, but a voice screamed up from the basement, "Cut that out up there, or your friend here gets it!"

Rabbi Saperstone stopped in his tracks!

At the bottom of the stairs, Papa Krasner hesitated.

"Where is it?" demanded the thief.

"It's too dark. I'm an old man. I can't see too good vere I put it."

"Quit stalling. I'm warning you for the last time!"

As Papa Krasner led the thief to the old stove, Rabbi Saperstone tried to hop more quietly, but his chair tilted backwards and he fell against the kitchen door. It slammed shut with a loud bang, and immediately, a large section of pipe fell down from the top of the furnace in the basement, landing directly on the thief's head and knocking him cold!

"Ve got him!" cried Papa Krasner. "Ve got him — de good-for-notink!"

He was so excited he almost forgot that Rabbi Saperstone was tied up. But once he remembered, he hurried upstairs, untied him, and then the two men returned to the basement to tie up the thief.

Papa Krasner pulled the thief's scarf down and exclaimed, "How do you like dat? It's de man vat drives de laundry truck to bring linen to de *shul*. Ven he came Monday morning, he must haf heard me tell de *shamash* I took de money home mit me. Dat good-for-notink!" he repeated.

"I think we should call the police right away, Mr. Krasner," said Rabbi Saperstone.

"Dat's right! Come, let's go."

As they climbed the stairs, they heard Miriam and Mama Krasner coming in the front door.

"Papa, where are you?" called Miriam. "We're back and Benny is here."

"Ve're here—coming up from de basement."

"Oy," groaned Miriam, "the basement . . ."

As Papa Krasner emerged from the basement, puffing from the ordeal, he said, "Benny, call de police. Ve gotta tief tied up in de basement."

"You what?" exclaimed three shocked voices in unison.

"You heard me. Call de police!"

Miriam ran down the stairs and right back up.

"He's right. They do. Call the police—quick!"

Benny called the police while Mama Krasner sat down, overwhelmed. Turning to her father, Miriam said, "I told you not to leave the money in the basement. How did you catch him?"

While Papa Krasner told them the story, including the very important point about how the old furnace had been instrumental in capturing the burglar, the police arrived and took the thief away.

"'You'll have to come to the station tomorrow to make a statement and press charges."

"We'll be there, officer," said Benny.

After the police left, Papa Krasner turned to his wife, harumphed a little, raised an eyebrow, adjusted his spectacles, and said, "You know, Mama, I been tinking. It's a good idea maybe ve should move closer to de children. Vat you tink?" And he harumphed again.

"*I* think it's a perfectly marvelous idea," said Miriam. She winked to her mother and handed her father a real estate contract, all typed out and ready to sign.

"Here, Papa," she said, "just write your name on the dotted line, and it will all be legal!"

❄ Green Mold

❄ It was a crisp, clear, September morning, and a steady breeze swept the trees clean of their multi-colored leaves. All was peaceful as Kenneth Abramsky tinkered with his car outside the big apartment building on Stetman Street. When he finally lowered the hood with a resounding slam, he saw his two-year-old son come out of the apartment building.

"Well, Ricky, old man, come to help your daddy fix the car?"

Ricky laughed and wrapped his arms around his father. Then he sat down on the curb while Kenneth slithered under the chassis of the car.

"Stay right there, Ricky . . . don't come under here."

Ricky squatted on the ground and watched his father's face disappear into the shadows under the car.

Phyllis Abramsky leaned out of the second-story apartment window and shouted for Ricky to come back upstairs. She was afraid Kenneth would be too absorbed in the car to watch the boy.

An alarm rang, shattering the heavy slumber of Mrs. Mathilda Bond. Drugged with sleep, she managed to roll over and stop the steady ringing of the noisy clock. She was old and weary; it was time for her to rest. But one couldn't live without money, and there was no money without work. So she forced her aged, thin body up into a sitting position and got out of the bed.

Her arthritis was bothering her again, and it was hard to move her arms. Slowly, she took her black-and-white checkered dress from the closet and started to dress.

At the other end of town, Pearl Brown was also awakened by an alarm. Pearl was young and healthy, but like Mrs. Bond, she, too, needed money. Pearl, however, shut off her clock, pulled the covers over her head, and went back to sleep.

When she woke once more and looked at the clock, it was 8:30. "Well, isn't that too bad! I went and missed the bus," she mused. "No use rushing now." She turned to the other side and pulled the comforter back over her head.

The Steinbergers lived in the apartment house on Stetman Street on the same floor as the Abramskys. That particular morning, Charna Steinberger rolled fitfully in bed. She didn't feel sick, yet she didn't feel well either. Perhaps it was the fast? No, it was too early in the morning to feel uncomfortable about that. Well, whatever it was, there was nothing to be done about it now. It was Yom Kippur, and she set her mind to thoughts of prayer and repentance.

She washed her hands, said the morning blessings, and walked sluggishly into her daughter Penina's room.

"Come, *bubbala*," she said. "Let's get you dressed. I want you to eat breakfast before Pearl gets here."

"Is Pearl going to be here all day?" asked the curly-haired, three-year-old girl.

"Yes, little one, but I'll try to walk home from the yeshiva in the afternoon to see how you are. It's Yom Kippur you know, and Mommy and Daddy have to *daven* very hard today."

A tall, bespectacled man came into the room.

"Charna, I'm leaving. When you come to the yeshiva let me know you've arrived."

"All right. Good *yom tov*."

"Good *yom tov*. Have an easy fast."

"You, too."

In the next apartment, Hindel Tepper finished feeding her twin sons and put them back to sleep. She dressed quickly and left food out for Mrs. Bond to eat during the day.

When the bus arrived, Mrs. Bond got off, and clutching her handbag under her arm, she slowly walked the two blocks to Hindel's apartment.

"Good morning, Mr. Abramsky," she said, as she passed the figure under the car.

Kenneth stuck his head out between the wheels.

"Why, hello there, Mrs. Bond. How are you today?"

"Oh, as well as can be expected, I guess."

"Have a good day," he said.

"The same to you," replied Mrs. Bond, as she entered the building.

Hindel was already out on the landing waiting for her.

"The twins are asleep, Mrs. Bond," said Hindel. "It's late and we have to run to the yeshiva. I left everything for you on the kitchen table. You know, it's Yom Kippur and I can't call you today, but I'll try to come home later on to see how everything is."

"Good-bye," said Mrs. Bond, climbing the stairs to the open door on the left.

Meanwhile, Charna Steinberger stood anxiously looking out the window, waiting for Pearl. The kitchen clock read 8:45.

"Mrs. Bond arrived. Maybe Pearl will be on the next bus," thought Charna to herself, beginning to wonder if she could climb the long hill to the yeshiva. She had begun to feel worse, but it was an undefined feeling. She really couldn't tell what was the matter. Nothing in particular hurt her. It was just a general feeling of misery.

As she sat nervously looking out the window, her glance fell on Kenneth Abramsky absorbed in his car. She couldn't help but think to herself, "Even on Yom Kippur. What a pity they don't even keep Yom Kippur."

Time passed slowly, and by 9:15, Charna had to

admit to herself that Pearl wasn't coming. She began to change Penina's clothes, intending to take her to the yeshiva.

"I probably won't be able to *daven* much with Penina there. But *davening* in *shul*—even if only a little—will still be better than staying home alone all day," she thought to herself.

"Can I take a cookie bag?" asked Penina.

"Not today, Peninaleh. You can't carry on Yom Kippur. Here let me . . . Oh! Oh . . ." Charna suddenly doubled over in pain.

"What's wrong, Mommy?"

"I don't know . . . my stomach . . ." Charna sank into the chair beside Penina's bed. "I have terrible pains in my stomach. Go and play a little until I feel better."

But Charna didn't feel better; she began to feel worse. Much worse. Several minutes passed and she became so weak that she wondered if she could stand up. With great effort she managed to rise. Her heart was pounding furiously. It seemed as if the whole room resounded with its heavy beat. She was wet with perspiration and was forced to lean against the wall to support herself. After a few moments, groping her way along the wall, Charna reached the door of the room. She didn't hear Penina, and she was too weak to call her. Edging her way slowly down the hall, she at last reached her bedroom and lay down on the bed. She lay for what seemed like hours, unable to move. The pains came and went, along with waves of nausea. She was feverish and then chilled, and then feverish again.

Penina wandered into the room. "When are we going, Mommy?" she asked, tugging at her mother's arm. Charna parted her lips but no sound came out.

"Mommy? Mommy, are you listening? When are we going?" came the insistent childish questioning.

"Mommy is sick," whispered Charna.

"What, Mommy? What did you say?"

Charna couldn't answer. The pain was back in her abdomen. All she could do was moan.

Penina, feeling ignored, went back to her favorite spot in the living room, her own rocking chair. Rocking back and forth she sang to herself and played.

When Charna opened her eyes, she didn't know whether she had slept or passed out. The pain had lessened, but the nausea and weakness were still there.

"Penina, where is Penina?" she thought. She tried to raise herself from the bed, but the room began to swim before her eyes. She lay back on the pillow.

Summoning every ounce of strength, she called out, "Penina! Come here, Penina."

Penina toddled into the room.

"She's all right. *Baruch Hashem*," thought Charna. "Penina," she said, "Mommy is very sick. Open the front door and leave it open. Go across the hall and knock on Hindel's door. Ask Mrs. Bond if she can take care of you for a while until Mommy feels better."

Always happy to go to Hindel's apartment and see the twins, Penina hurried off to do as she was told. She knocked on the door, and in a few moments, the kindly Mrs. Bond appeared.

"Hello there, honey. What can I do for you?"

Penina carefully relayed the message. Mrs. Bond immediately took her by the hand and hurried in to see Charna.

Pressing her hand against Charna's forehead, Mrs. Bond exclaimed, "Oh, you're hot! My, but you're hot!" Mrs. Bond touched Charna's hand. "You feel clammy. I think we'd better call your husband right now."

"You can't, Mrs. Bond. It's our High Holy Day. No one will answer the phone at the yeshiva."

"Well, you can't stay here by yourself. Maybe I should call an ambulance."

"No, no, no," said Charna. "Please, just watch Penina for me. Maybe if I sleep a little, then I'll feel better."

"You're burning up, honey. You shouldn't be here alone, and I've got to stay with the twins. Let me get you something cold to drink."

"No, thank you. I can't eat or drink today. It's Yom Kippur, a fast day. Please, Mrs. Bond, just watch Penina," pleaded Charna wearily and closed her eyes. It was hard for her to talk, and she soon fell asleep.

When she awoke, Phyllis Abramsky was standing over her bed.

"What is this? Grand Central Station?" thought Charna irritably. Immediately, she regretted her unkind thoughts. They were only trying to help.

"Look, Charna, Mrs. Bond told me you're not well. Even though we don't fast, I do know that it's Yom Kippur. But you're awfully sick with something, and your husband should be here. Maybe under the circumstances you'd be allowed to drink something or take an aspirin, or call a doctor."

"No," insisted Charna, "I'll be all right. Please, just watch my baby."

"Then I'll send Kenneth up to the yeshiva to bring your husband home."

"Oh, no," said Charna, "I don't want anyone to ride on Yom Kippur because of me. No, definitely not! Please, just let me rest."

She was too weak to argue any more, and she felt so hot, so very hot. Phyllis felt her head and then left.

Half an hour later, Charna tried to sit up again. This time she was successful. After remaining in a sitting position for several moments, she tried to stand.

"*Baruch Hashem*," she said. "Now, if I can just wash my hands for *netilas yadayim*, maybe I can get to the living room and *daven* a little."

Her desire to pray was so strong that, despite her fever and weakness, she managed to do as she had planned, but the walk to the living room completely exhausted her. She leaned against the back of the couch, unable to move. Then there was a knock at the door, and Phyllis and Kenneth came in. Charna couldn't believe her eyes — Kenneth had a yarmulke on his head!

"Look, I put on this yarmulke, and as you can see," he said, turning his pockets inside out, "I'm not carrying anything in my pockets. Now, I don't care how much you protest, but I am going to walk to the yeshiva and get your husband."

"But it's so far. I'll be all right."

"You look awful, and I'm going!" With that, Kenneth left the apartment and began his long walk to the yeshiva. Although Kenneth felt timid about entering a house of worship after all these years, he felt that he had no choice, since it was obviously necessary to call Charna's husband.

He paused at the bottom of the half-mile hill leading up to the yeshiva. The heavy traffic was noisy down here in the streets, but further up, all was still. Kenneth took a deep breath and started climbing. As he neared the top, he heard the swell of voices rising in unison. It drowned out the noise of the traffic completely. The sound of voices raised in prayer to their Creator sent a chill through his spine and tugged at his heart. The beauty, the great awe in those voices so stunned him, that he was unable to move. Kenneth was filled with sorrow and longing—a longing for that truth which he had left so many years before. He was drawn as if by some giant magnet toward those inspiring voices. The closer he came, the more intense was his turmoil. When he reached the door of the *beis midrash*, he was trembling and tears clouded his eyes.

He stood at the door and saw hundreds of *tallis*-clad worshipers pouring out their hearts to God. At that moment, something changed in Kenneth Abramsky, and he was never the same again.

Charna's husband, Josh, hurriedly walked down the long-winding road beside Kenneth. Both were absorbed in thought; Josh was deeply concerned about his wife, while Kenneth was deeply concerned about himself.

Reaching the apartment, they found Charna resting on the couch. Josh immediately insisted on calling an ambulance, but Charna refused.

"But it's perfectly permissible. I asked the *rav* before I left the yeshiva."

"No, no . . . I'm still in pain, but I really am feeling much better than I was before, and if I didn't call for help then, there is certainly no need to call now."

Kenneth did whatever else he could to help and then went home, leaving Josh to take care of his wife. As the hours passed, Charna felt better and better. By evening, the pain in her stomach had lessened and the fever had gone down. The feeling of weakness, however, was overwhelming, a result of fasting and the illness.

When Yom Kippur was over, Josh telephoned the doctor.

"Sounds like food poisoning," speculated Dr. Manuel. "Ask your wife what she ate yesterday."

"The regular, two big meals we always eat before Yom Kippur. And I also opened a can of tuna late in the afternoon for a nosh," answered Charna.

"Well, she seems to be holding her own at the present," said the doctor. "Let her rest, eat a bland diet, and drink lots of water. Have her see me first thing in the morning. If you have any tuna left, take a look at it," instructed Dr. Manuel. "It seems to be the only thing your wife ate that the rest of you didn't."

Josh thanked the doctor and hung up the phone. Then he opened the refrigerator and looked at the tuna. It was covered with spots of green mold.

Charna was soon feeling much better, and when the Abramskys asked if they could come for a Friday night meal, Charna and Josh were more than happy to have them.

That *erev Shabbos* the Abramskys arrived early to watch Charna light candles. Phyllis had never owned a pair of candlesticks and had never lit Shabbos candles.

"Charna," she asked, "explain whatever you do tonight. Kenneth knows about these things, but I don't, and I don't want to do anything wrong."

"Of course. I'll be happy to."

It was a beautiful evening, and the Abramskys basked in the warmth and glow of the Shabbos. Their faces were radiant. For the first time, they spoke about themselves and their backgrounds to the Steinbergers.

"Until I was eighteen," said Kenneth, "I was observant. I had a very traditional upbringing, but then, several things happened which changed everything. It was a very hard time for me, and I still don't like to talk about it."

"Your past is your own business, Kenneth, but we're happy that we can give you a chance to enjoy something you've missed for so many years," said Josh.

Kenneth sang the *zemiros* in his beautiful baritone voice, giving as much pleasure to the Steinbergers as he received from them. This was the first of many such Shabbos invitations, until eventually, the Abramskys began to keep the Shabbos in their own home.

And all because of green mold!

✳ *Down the Drain*

✳ "I don't think you should tell Miss Bailey."

"Well, I have to. She'll find out anyway."

"Maybe you can fake it. Then she'll never know."

"Nope. Honesty is the best policy."

"But she'll give you a 'C' and you'll ruin your average."

"We'll see. There's the bell—I'll meet you after school!" said Naomi to her friend Esther as she slammed the steel-gray locker door and raced into Room 256. Sliding into her seat behind the long lab table, she ran a hand through her curly auburn hair and mulled over the problem of how to approach Miss Bailey.

Battle-ax Bailey, as she was usually called, was formidable, to say the least, and the ninth graders tended to cringe at the mere mention of her name. She was almost six feet tall and six feet wide, with muscles like a man. It was wagered that she weighed close to three hundred pounds; she had to enter the doorway sideways, but everyone was afraid to laugh.

Her voice matched her body—hoarse and booming—and she always gave orders instead of listening to what anyone else had to say. She liked to talk, or rather *yell*, about the good old days when she had been a nutritionist in the navy during World War II. The girls in her home economics class often felt as though they were swabbing decks in the navy instead of washing counters in the home ec. room.

"So," thought Naomi, "how do you talk to someone like that? Better yet, how do you talk about something as important as *kashrus* to someone who doesn't listen?"

Being one of only four religious girls in a high school of a thousand students often presented problems, but Naomi had been taught at home, *"lefum tza'ara agra"*—reward is in proportion to one's suffering. So she dealt with each problem as it presented itself, and the result was that both her Jewish and her gentile classmates respected and admired her devotion to Judaism.

But Naomi envied her younger sister and brother who were attending the new Jewish day school. When the day school movement first began in Boston, it was too late for Naomi, who was already in high school, to attend. Years ago, her parents had engaged a private tutor for her after the only afternoon Hebrew school in town had closed, and she still studied three times a week with Mr. Fayer. Her father tested her every Shabbos to make sure her progress was satisfactory.

But to Naomi's mind, it still wasn't the same as being in a Jewish day school. How she yearned for that! Then she wouldn't have to deal with people like Miss Bailey.

It was too bad Miss Bailey taught her the last period. Now she would have to spend the entire day worrying what to do. If only there were some way to get out of cooking class; but state law required her to attend.

So, "that was that" as Mr. Thompson, the vice-principal, had put it to her parents, Mr. and Mrs. Stein.

"Naomi, name the bones of the hand," called Mrs. Smith.

"Pardon me?"

"Aren't you paying attention?"

"I'm sorry. Could you please repeat the question?"

"Name the bones of the hand, please."

"Um—the carpal bones, metacarpal bones, and phalanges."

Soon the bell rang. As Naomi headed out the door to her algebra class, she felt a tug on her shoulder bag and turned to see Ruthie Weiss walking beside her.

"That's the second time in two days Smith has caught you off guard. What's the matter? It's not like you."

"I don't know. All I can think about is having to talk to Miss Bailey. It's driving me crazy. I'm scared of her, but I have to say *something* before we really start cooking."

"I think Esther's right. Why don't you just fake it? Who can talk to Bailey?"

"No. I have to be straightforward about it. It will come out in the end anyway, and then I'll look dishonest, and besides, I'm not doing anything wrong. *She* is!"

"That may be, but I don't think you'll win, and it'll spoil your average. Over a class like cooking yet! And then, there goes your scholastic award. Well, it's your decision. See you at lunch," said Ruthie as she turned off to her English class.

Naomi hurried down to the second floor for algebra. The morning dragged on through history and English, until finally it was lunchtime. Naomi climbed the stairs to the fourth-floor annex to get her lunch and made her way to the enormous cafeteria that extended half-way across the fourth floor. She went to her regular table and found her friends, Esther and Ruthie, already there.

Naomi opened her lunch bag and took out her tuna fish sandwich, a double-size piece of chocolate cake and an apple.

"Ummmm — good lunch," commented Naomi.

"How can you think about food at a time like this?" said Esther. "If I were you I'd be sick to my stomach."

"Look, I'm hungry, so please don't ruin my meal," retorted Naomi. "I'm worried, but starving myself won't make it any better. Anyway, I've made up my mind to talk to her before class, and I think I know what I'm going to say."

"What? Let's hear."

Naomi nervously twisted her napkin. "I think I'd rather not say anything now. It might be better if I just blurt it out at the right time. Come on; let's wash and eat so we can take a walk before lunchtime is over."

The three girls strolled along the path near the annex for the last ten minutes of their lunch period. Ruthie and Esther were both deeply concerned about their friend's decision. They felt she was taking a big chance in trying to reason with Battle-ax Bailey. Naomi, on the other hand, continued to waver between feeling courageous and quivering with fear.

As the hands of the clock crept toward 2:15, Naomi went over her speech in her mind once again. Books in hand, she approached the huge Home Economics Room. There Miss Bailey stood in front of the door as usual. Her cropped black hair was covered with a hairnet, and a large, white chef's apron covered the purple-and-white print dress she wore every Monday. Her voice shaking slightly, Naomi began, "Miss Bailey, could I speak to you for a moment?"

"The bell is about to ring. No time to talk now."

"But it's very important. It's about class."

"Just do your work and you'll pass."

"No. It has to do with something else," insisted Naomi.

"After class, after class. Sit down *now!*"

The "now" convinced Naomi to sit down. She was frustrated and angry. "What kind of person is she? She won't even let you say something!" she thought to herself.

The entire class period was spent cleaning counter tops again and reviewing table setting, neither of which was very interesting. Naomi became angrier and

angrier, and when the class was finally over, she was so angry that she momentarily forgot to be frightened.

"Miss Bailey, I must talk to you."

"Class is over," boomed Bailey.

"I know, Miss Bailey, but you said I could talk to you after class, and now it's after class."

"Then out with it. I'm in a hurry. I want to go home too, you know."

Naomi was so exasperated that she just blurted out, "I'm an Orthodox Jew, and in our home we keep the Jewish dietary laws. That means I can't eat any of the food we cook in class."

"If you don't eat, you get a 'C.' If you do poorly on anything else, you fail. Those are the rules."

"But, Miss Bailey, it's against my religion. I can't do it."

"I've heard plenty of excuses in my time, and using religion won't get you anywhere. No exceptions. You don't eat, you get a 'C.' You do poorly on anything else, you fail. You're excused!"

Tears welled up in Naomi's dark brown eyes. Her heart was pounding from anger and frustration as she stumbled away from the huge purple-and-white figure. Esther, Ruthie and Shirley were at the flagpole, waiting for her as she came out of the school building, clutching her books and blinking away the tears.

"It was bad, huh?" asked Esther.

"Don't worry, maybe something will come up to change it," suggested Shirley.

"Come on, we'll walk you home," said Ruthie.

The four friends walked slowly up Beacon Street

and to Naomi's house. Mrs. Stein was in the kitchen baking. She greeted the girls, smiling cheerfully until she saw her daughter's face.

"She said 'no.' Right?"

"Oh, Mama, she wouldn't even listen to me. She's horrible!"

"Naomi, this isn't the first time something is difficult for you and it won't be the last, but *Hashem* will help. You just try and do what's right. Believe me, Naomele, I know how you feel, but it will work itself out," said Mrs. Stein, her heart aching for her daughter. She placed an arm around Naomi's shoulder and planted a loving kiss on her tear-stained cheek. The girls stayed for a while to cheer up their friend. Before leaving, they promised to try and devise some way of solving the problem.

That night Naomi didn't sleep very well. She had a terrible nightmare. She dreamt that Miss Bailey was holding her by the chin trying to force a spoonful of gravy down her throat. Naomi couldn't budge from the spot or even scream. She finally awoke and, trembling, crept down to the kitchen to make herself a glass of tea.

The next afternoon was the first day of actual cooking. The girls were going to bake cookies and make hot chocolate. The home economics class was in a very large, rectangular room, painted green. It contained several sets of sinks along one side, and two refrigerators and more sinks along the back wall. The third side was all windows, and the teacher's desk and the blackboard were at the front. The middle of the room was filled with enormous four-burner stoves and ten working areas. Four girls were assigned to each counter and half a stove. As the girls entered the room, each was told to draw a slip of paper with the number of her assignment.

Naomi hurriedly drew her slip and avoided looking at Miss Bailey. She opened the paper and saw 10-2, indicating counter ten, seat 2. "Wonderful," thought Naomi, "at least I'll be as far away from her desk as possible."

The girls sat down, and Naomi found herself at a table with Joan Cassidy, Barbara Dimling, and Kathy Marcelli. These girls, all non-Jews, had known Naomi since junior high and had always been friendly. They knew of Naomi's problem and sympathized with her.

"We heard you approached Battle-ax Bailey yesterday," said Joan. "Was she true to form? 'You don't eat, you get a 'C'; you do anything else wrong, you fail!'"

"She sure was," sighed Naomi.

"I wish there was something we could do to help. She's really nasty and it's so unfair," said Joan.

"Maybe there *is* something we can do," said Barbara with a big smile on her face. "I've got an idea. We could eat your food for you! I don't mind eating extra chocolate-chip cookies."

"Say, that's a great idea. We could split up your cocoa too, and she would never know the difference," said Katy.

"I'm not so sure about that," said Naomi cautiously. "She must come back to check, and I don't want you to get into trouble. It's bad enough I have a problem."

"Listen, I heard she only comes back here the first day and maybe once or twice a semester," continued Barbara, "because the room is so long. She's so big and it's hard for her to move around a lot. Marilyn Magee had her last semester, and she told me to try to get a back stove for just that reason. Besides, we'd like to help you out. You've always helped us with our algebra. Now we can do something for you."

"That's right," agreed Kathy.

"Count me in," said Joan.

"Gee, thanks a lot," said Naomi, trying to hold back her tears. "That's really good of you. But are you sure you want to do this? I don't want anyone to get into trouble because of me."

"Quiet!" boomed Miss Bailey's voice across the room. "Or I'll have you scrubbing sinks after school."

"Sh . . . it's settled," whispered Barbara.

Naomi was so happy she thought she would burst. Her mother's words ran through her mind, 'You do what is right and *Hashem* will help.' "He really did help," rejoiced Naomi.

Barbara and Naomi set up the mix-master and got to work on their recipe. Soon the room was abuzz with the sound of whirring motors, banging pans and clattering utensils. The windows clouded from the warm oven vapor, and the smell of freshly baked cookies filled the halls of Markham High.

"Clean-up time," yelled the gruff voice. "Set your tables to eat!" Everyone scurried to and fro, scrubbing tables, cleaning spatulas and measuring cups, and finally sitting down to eat.

"Hurry up, everyone, let's eat fast," whispered Barbara.

Joan poured four full cups of cocoa. Then each girl drank hers and refilled her cup from Naomi's. They finished the dozen cookies without any difficulty, leaving a cookie and some cocoa in the pot for Miss Bailey to see before they cleared the table. They were finished with everything and ready for inspection by the time Miss Bailey reached table six. Naomi held her breath as she watched Miss Bailey waddle slowly toward her end of the stove. She walked directly to Naomi and picked up her cup. Only a residue of cocoa remained on the very bottom.

"I thought you'd come around when you saw you couldn't get away with it. Keeping kosher as an excuse—ha!"

Naomi's cheeks burned with anger. "Boy, just wait until the semester is over," she thought to herself, "I'm going to come back and tell you a thing or two, if you don't find out before. I'm going to tell you exactly what we did and what I think of you!"

The days passed, and true to Barbara's words, Miss Bailey rarely made it to the back of the room. Everyone pitied the girls who were unlucky enough to be sitting at tables one through three. She sat over them like a hawk, always criticizing, always yelling.

Occasionally, the routine of the class was broken by a film or slides, and by the middle of the semester, Naomi felt quite complacent. After all, everything had been going so well this far. What could go wrong now?

One snowy afternoon, the girls came into home

economics, picked up their assignments, and settled down to work.

"What did we get this time?" asked Kathy.

"Corn soup," answered Joan.

"Corn soup! What in the world is that?"

"I don't know. Soup made out of corn, I guess. Doesn't sound very appetizing, does it?"

"No. Sure doesn't. Well, let's get started," said Kathy.

The girls took out the pots and measured the corn and water.

"I think ours looks too watery," said Barbara. "Let's add more flour."

"OK," said Naomi. "How much? About half a cup?"

"I don't know. That seems like too much. Put in a quarter of a cup."

Naomi measured out a quarter of a cup and added it to the mixture. She stirred it around and nothing happened.

"Put some more in," said Joan. "It still looks watery. I don't like these recipes where they say, 'add enough to thicken.' How do you know how much is enough?"

"Let's just keep mixing and see what happens," offered Barbara.

"We've been mixing it, and nothing has happened. Naomi, measure out another half a cup of flour and put it in," directed Joan.

"That will be almost two cups of flour altogether. Don't you think it will be flour soup instead of corn soup?" laughed Naomi. The girls deliberated a while longer and decided to add another half a cup of flour.

"I don't understand why nothing is cooking," said Barbara. "Since we poured in the first cup of flour, it stopped bubbling. How come?"

"That's right," remarked Joan. "It was bubbling and then it stopped. Maybe the flour is too thick to bubble."

"Boy, are we ever dumb," Barbara fairly shouted all of a sudden. "We spilled so much flour out, we snuffed out the gas flame. No wonder it stopped bubbling. Someone go get a match."

Kathy brought a match and relit the gas, and soon the mixture on the stove began to bubble. It bubbled and boiled until it became too thick to stir.

"Do you think we ought to add some more water?" asked Naomi. "It's beginning to look like dough instead of soup."

"It's almost up to the top of the pot already. If we add water, it'll overflow," said Joan.

"Let's pour it into a bigger pot," said Naomi.

"We can't," answered Kathy.

"Why not?"

"Because this is already the biggest pot we have."

"Well, it sure doesn't look like soup, and I don't even see any corn in it, so let's add some more water. It can't get worse than it is already," said Barbara, to which they all agreed.

Naomi added another cup of water and soon the thick liquid hissed and sputtered and erupted from the pot, rolling down the sides, over the grates and into the flames.

"Quick! Shut off the gas before we start a fire!" Joan cried.

"We can't! The recipe says it has to cook ten minutes more," said Kathy.

"If we cook it ten minutes more, it'll be all over the stove instead of in the pot," Naomi whispered.

"But you can't eat it raw!" Barbara insisted.

"Who can eat this at all?" retorted Joan.

Suddenly Naomi had a sick feeling in the pit of her stomach. "Who can eat this at all?" she wondered. "They probably won't want to eat theirs, so who is going to eat mine? Oh boy! Bailey hasn't been to our table in weeks. Just watch . . . I have this funny feeling that she'll pick *today* to come by!"

Soon the directive came. "All hands clear the tables! Set up to eat!" The girls cleaned up and then cautiously divided the "soup" into four bowls.

"Well, who's brave enough to taste this goop?" asked Joan.

They looked at each other, then at the soup, and then back at each other.

"Give me a dollar and I'll poison myself first," joked Barbara.

"Not funny!" thought Naomi.

"Well, I may as well start," said Barbara as she gingerly lifted the spoon to her mouth. She rolled the thick mush slowly around over her tongue. She made a face and promptly spit the mouthful into her napkin.

"Yuk! You could *die* from this! I can't eat it. *It's awful!*"

"Let's see," said Joan, licking the tip of her spoon. "Ick! It *is* pretty bad."

"Do you think it could really make us sick?" wondered Kathy. "After all, everything in it is edible." She stuck her finger into the bowl and examined the mixture. She licked her finger and promptly gagged.

"Sorry, Naomi," she said. "You're going to have to suffer along with the rest of us today. I don't intend to eat mine, so I couldn't possibly eat yours."

The others nodded in agreement.

"We know it will be worse for you if you don't eat it because she has it in for you. We're sorry, honestly we are," said Barbara.

"I know. It's OK. Maybe I'll dump it down the sink when she isn't looking."

"There is no way you can get up without her seeing you go to the sink. Forget it!"

Miss Bailey started her slow waddle from group to group when there was a knock on the door.

"Come in," she boomed.

"Excuse me, Miss Bailey," said one of the school secretaries, "there is an important phone call for you in the office. Could you come right away?"

"Everyone will stay seated and quiet until I return. Understood?" boomed Battle-ax Bailey as she headed out the door.

The minute she left the room, Naomi grabbed her bowl of soup and dashed toward the sink. Shaking, she emptied the sticky mixture down the drain and turned on the hot water faucet, but the hot water came out cold and the porridge was only partially dissolved in the drain.

"There's no hot water. What should I do?" called Naomi to her group.

"Let it run. It'll get hot and then we can empty ours too."

Naomi turned the faucet on full force, but no hot water came out. Instead, cold water began to collect in the sink because the drain was clogged with the thick flour mixture.

"Here she comes," cried someone from the front of the room. "Naomi, hurry up and sit down."

Naomi turned off the faucet and dashed to her seat. She managed to reach her chair just as the door opened. Miss Bailey shuffled to table four where she had left off and continued her inspection.

There were still fifteen minutes until the bell — time enough for Miss Bailey to reach the last group and the back sink. "Too much time," thought Naomi, feeling shaky, "too much time."

Miss Bailey was now at table eight. "You call this pot clean?" she boomed. "My shoes are cleaner than this pot! You and your partner — to the back sink! I want to see you scrub this pot clean — now!"

The whole class gasped. Everyone had seen Naomi throw her food down the sink. One of the girls from table eight started to walk to a side sink and the others followed her lead.

"The back sink, I said," came a rasping voice. "Can't you hear? I said the back sink!"

Slowly the girls moved toward the back sink, hoping the bell would ring. Unfortunately, there was still plenty of time until dismissal. One girl found the cleanser while another took the steel wool.

"Well," shouted Miss Bailey. "What are you waiting for? Turn on the water."

85]

Slowly, the water began to rise in the sink. Small pieces of yellow corn began floating to the top of the pasty-colored mixture. Everyone froze as Miss Bailey walked to the back and peered into the stuffed sink. She turned off the water.

"All right," bellowed the teacher, "who is the culprit who spilled her soup down the sink? Stand up now!"

Naomi's heart began to beat like a drum. She was sure the whole room could hear it. Her knees felt like rubber and a sinking feeling in the pit of her stomach made her think she was going to faint.

The room was silent. Everyone's eyes were on Miss Bailey. Naomi put her right hand on the counter for support as she tried to stand up. Barbara and Kathy saw her move.

Suddenly, Naomi felt a hand on each of her knees as the two girls forced her to remain seated in her place. She wanted to speak out, but fear prevented her from uttering a sound. Everyone in the class knew who the "culprit" was, but no one said anything. The class was silent.

"Well, then, we will summon Mr. Hackman, the plumber, and this entire class will remain after school until the work is finished, unless, of course, the guilty party will speak up and spare her classmates."

Miss Bailey lumbered out of the classroom to call Mr. Hackman. As the door closed behind her, the girls started to whisper from all corners of the room:

"Don't tell, Naomi."

"She's so unfair! We'll stand by you!"

"Don't say anything, Naomi. She tried to make you go against your religion."

"We don't mind staying after."

"She'll never find out from us."

Naomi was so overwhelmed, she couldn't reply. Only the look on her face expressed what she was feeling.

When the door opened, the girls became silent. The only sound was the clank of Mr. Hackman's wrench as he removed the pipe. They all watched the thick goo drip slowly into the bucket beneath the sink.

"Somebody sure ain't such a good cook," chuckled Mr. Hackman.

Nobody thought it was funny. A while later Mr. Hackman left.

"Still won't tell, will you?" boomed Miss Bailey. "Well, that will cost each and every one of you a five-hundred word essay for tomorrow on the purpose of cooking class. Dismissed!"

Worn out from the tension and feeling shaky, Naomi left the room and the school with reassurances of loyalty from all her sympathetic friends. Once safely at home, she burst into tears. Her mother, while trying to comfort her, decided she would speak to her husband that evening. Something had to be done.

That night after dinner, Mr. and Mrs. Stein sat up late in the kitchen, discussing Naomi's plight.

"I don't see what going back to the school will do. We've already talked to the vice-principal."

"Then maybe this time we should go to the princi-pal himself. The whole situation has gotten out of hand. The child may fail, and then she'll have to go through another semester in the same situation with the same teacher. And now that the entire class was punished because of her, there is bound to be resentment."

"You're right," said Mr. Stein. "We must take a stand. Poor Naomi. We'll go first thing in the morning, on my way to work."

"Good," replied Mrs. Stein, sounding more definite than she felt. She didn't really know what to expect.

Early the following morning, Naomi and her parents walked into Mr. MacGregor's office. She had never been there before. No one ever saw much of Mr. MacGregor except at assemblies or official school functions. Disciplinary action and other school matters all seemed to be taken care of by Mr. Thompson, so everyone looked upon Mr. MacGregor with awe. His office was cheery enough. Naomi had expected it to resemble a dungeon of sorts. Not only was she surprised by the decor, but three of her friends were standing at Mr. MacGregor's desk—Ruth, Esther and Shirley! And they all were smiling.

"Good morning, Mr. MacGregor," said Mr. Stein as he shook the principal's hand.

"And a very good morning to you, sir. I understand you have somewhat of a problem. These three young ladies came very early this morning to speak to me about your daughter," said Mr. MacGregor, indicating the girls. "She must be a very special person to be worthy of such loyal friendship and to have the backing and respect of all her classmates."

"Why, thank you, Mr. MacGregor. I see you have been informed of the situation which brought me here this morning," answered Mr. Stein.

"Yes, I have. I am sorry that it was not brought to my attention sooner. I'm a religious man myself, sir. In a public school certain standards must be maintained, and we cannot be lenient in excusing students from state and federal regulations. In your case, however, I certainly think we have a very legitimate exception to the rule, and I will see to it that Naomi will be legally excused from partaking of the food."

"Thank you so much for your understanding and your time, Mr. MacGregor," said Mrs. Stein. "If I may, I'd just like to ask one more question."

"Certainly."

"Will this affect Naomi's grade and classroom treatment?"

"Absolutely not. I intend to speak to Miss Bailey before the day is out."

Then, turning to Naomi with a smile, he added, "Now, don't worry, young lady. Everything will be all right."

The little group left Mr. MacGregor's office in a distinctly happier mood than they had entered.

"Whatever made you girls do a thing like that?" asked Naomi.

"Wouldn't you have done the same for us?" asked Ruth.

"What kind of friends would we be if we didn't try to help?" said Shirley.

"And especially," said Esther, "if we *frum* girls

don't stick up for each other when it comes to *Yiddish-keit*, who will? But you were lucky, Naomi. You had *all* the girls in class supporting you."

"We can't thank you enough," said Mrs. Stein.

"Let's celebrate today at my house," said Esther.

"Great idea," said Shirley.

"We'll meet at the flagpole after school," said Ruth.

"Well, I've got to get to work. I want to thank you all again for your help," said Mr. Stein.

"Just a minute, Chaim," said Mrs. Stein, "I'll save you a trip. Since the girls are going to Esther's house, they can take the copy of our cookbook to Esther's mother and then you'll be free to go straight to work."

"Wonderful. I'll be right back with it." Mr. Stein hurried out to the parking lot.

"Oh, it came!" exclaimed Naomi excitedly. "How does it look?"

"I think it's marvelous. I just want to get my co-chairman's opinion before I give the printer the go-ahead."

"Why didn't you tell me it came?"

"With all your troubles, I forgot to mention it." Turning to Esther, Mrs. Stein said, "Your mother is going to be surprised because I didn't have a chance to tell her either. Listen, Esther," she continued, "tell your mother how much I enjoyed working with her on the cookbook. I know the yeshiva will raise a lot of money selling it. It's really good. Have her call me this evening and let me know what she thinks."

"Sure thing, Mrs. Stein. Well, there goes the bell. I've got to get to the fourth floor."

"I'll see you later, then," said Naomi. "My first class is right down the hall so I'll wait for my father to bring the cookbook."

"OK. 'Bye, Mrs. Stein."

"So long."

"Good-bye and thanks again, girls," answered Mrs. Stein.

As her three friends left, Naomi confided to her mother, "Ma, I'm scared to go to Bailey's class this afternoon. She'll be angry."

"I thought of that. That's why I mentioned it to Mr. MacGregor. Look, we'll take it one step at a time. Go to class today and we'll see what happens. Good luck, Naomele."

At that moment, Mr. Stein returned to the building with the book. He handed it to Naomi and, after reassuring her once more, he and Mrs. Stein left while Naomi went to her first-period class.

All day Naomi worried about how Miss Bailey would react. She dreaded walking into class. Of course, by lunchtime, the news that Miss Bailey had been called to Mr. MacGregor's office had spread through the school like wildfire. Naomi could barely taste her food.

Finally, it was time for home economics. Naomi couldn't bring herself to enter the room alone. When Kathy and Barbara came along, she walked in between the two other girls.

In the back of the room, two men stood speaking with Miss Bailey. When everyone was seated, Miss Bailey introduced them. "Mr. Carnes is from the Board of Education, and Mr. Miller is a representative of the local Dairy Association. They are our guests for the period, and they have prepared a film which is being shown in all the schools. You will follow them to the second-floor annex for a special viewing, after which you will return here before dismissal. Leave all your things here. You may take only your purses. Everyone line up and follow these two gentlemen."

The class was soon walking down the hallway while Miss Bailey remained in the room. She moved slowly to the last table and sat down behind the counter, wondering how to fill her spare time. Her eyes wandered about the room and eventually fell on the pile of books stacked on one of the tables. A crisp red-and-white book, entitled "Kosher Kitchen," was on top of the pile. Out of curiosity, Miss Bailey leaned across the table and picked up the book. She flipped through the pages and then started reading the introduction entitled, "Hows and Whys of Keeping a Kosher Kitchen," by Mrs. C. Stein.

She was still reading when the class returned. As the girls sat down, she got up and walked over to Naomi, book in hand. "Did you ever eat this?" she asked, pointing to a recipe for *cholent*.

"Sure," answered Naomi nervously. "We eat it every Saturday for our Sabbath meal."

"You let it cook all night long?" she asked. "According to this, it cooks almost twenty-four hours. What in the world does it taste like? Why do you let it cook so long?"

"It's delicious," said Naomi, and thinking fast, she

added, "We aren't allowed to cook on the Sabbath. It's considered work, and the Bible commands us to rest on the Sabbath. So we make it the day before and leave it on the fire all night until we eat it. Maybe my mother could make you some in the middle of week so that you could taste it."

"Do you *really* keep all these religious rules?" asked Miss Bailey wonderingly.

"Yes, we do," said Naomi firmly and with conviction. "And as I said, I'm sure my mother will be happy to make you a sample of the *cholent*. If you want I can get you a copy of the cookbook after they're all printed. This is just a test copy sent to my mother for approval."

Instead of answering, Miss Bailey turned to the class and yelled, "Dismissed!" Everyone, including Naomi, hurried out.

Naomi met her friends at the flagpole and went with a light heart to Esther's house. Afterwards, she hurried home to tell her mother what had happened during cooking class.

"But I still don't know how she feels," said Naomi to her mother. "She didn't answer me."

"Maybe she didn't know what to say. After all, she was put on the spot today by her students and had to answer to the principal, so let's be nice about it and show her it wasn't malice, but a protection of our own religious freedom. I'm going to make her a *cholent*. Your idea was very good. Start peeling potatoes, my dear child."

Early the next morning, for the second time that

week, Mr. Stein drove Naomi to school. She went upstairs, carefully carrying the aluminum foil pan that
held the piping-hot *cholent*. She knocked on Miss
Bailey's door.

"Good morning, Miss Bailey. Here is the *cholent* I
told you about. All you need to do is keep it warm on
the fire until lunchtime. I hope you enjoy it."

Naomi placed the pan before the teacher and
watched as her eyes lit up at the tantalizing aroma. It
did smell good and she *did* like to eat. Naomi thought
that she saw a flicker of a smile on Battle-ax's face. She
wasn't really sure, because she couldn't remember
having ever seen Miss Bailey smile before.

"Where do you eat your lunch every day—in the
cafeteria?" Miss Bailey finally asked.

"I eat there, Miss Bailey, but I bring my lunch from
home," said Naomi, holding up her lunch bag to prove
it. "I told you, we keep kosher."

"I guess you really do keep kosher," came the reply.

As the jubilant Naomi left the room, she thought to
herself, "Everything is going to be all right. Yes, sireee,
everything is going to be all right—*baruch Hashem*!"

❄ Stranded

❄ The Rubens, worn out from the day's travel, sat listlessly in their stifling car. Daniel lay sleeping on the back seat, his damp head on his sister's lap. He stirred and shifted his position, to the chagrin of his sister, Chani.

"He's all wet," she complained.

"We're all hot and tired," answered Mrs. Ruben. "It's only another fifteen or twenty miles until we get there, so let's make the best of it."

Frayda, the oldest child, who was sitting in the back of the station wagon, commented for the third time in thirty minutes, "We should have had the air-conditioning fixed in the car. No two ways about it."

"There is nothing to be done about it now, so as your mother said, make the best of it," said her father. "It's not that bad."

The Rubens were on their way to Seattle to visit Mrs. Ruben's parents. They lived far away, and visiting was difficult, but they made the trip every summer. Since the plane fare was so expensive, they traveled by car. Even though the ride was exhausting, it was well worth it to see the happy faces of the grandparents when they arrived. It was a true *mitzva* of *kibbud av va'em* — honoring one's parents.

They were making fairly good speed when Mr. Ruben said, "That camper has been right behind us since the last rest stop. It's funny that they haven't passed us once."

"I know," said Frayda. "Every time I look out back, their kids wave to me. We have this real relationship going."

She pulled her sailor cap down over her ears and shifted her position, so her legs wouldn't fall asleep. She was really too big to sit in the back, but she preferred sitting alone to being all cramped and crowded in the back seat.

Daniel woke up and sat up, pushing his damp hair away from his face and adjusting his yarmulke.

"I'm thirsty. Can I have more water, please?" he asked.

"Again???" exclaimed Chani. "No, you can't. You were sleeping and you have to wash your hands before you can make a *bracha*. You'll have to wait until we get to the motel."

"But I'm thirsty," he complained.

"Well, you can't have any."

"Yes, he can, Chani," said Mrs. Ruben. "He only dozed off for a few minutes. You have to sleep at least half an hour before you must wash your hands. Just a minute, Daniel, I'll get you some," she said as she leaned over and lifted the water jug from beside her feet. She pulled out a plastic cup from the box beside her and poured some water into the cup. Carefully passing the cup to the back seat, she said, "There you are. Don't forget a *bracha*."

"I want a cookie, too," said Daniel.

"No, I don't think so," said Mrs. Ruben. "It will only make you thirstier and we don't have too much water left. We'll eat supper soon."

"It will be longer than that because we have to unpack first," replied Frayda, "and I'm starved, too."

"I'll tell you what. You'll all help Daddy unload and meanwhile I'll set up the food. It won't take long. I'm also hungry. It's almost seven hours since we ate lunch."

"No, it won't be long now," said Mr. Ruben as he pointed to the sign on the road. "Only twenty miles to Greenville."

"That's not far," murmured his wife.

"That camper is still behind us, and now there's a diesel truck in front of us and it's downhill all the way," commented Mr. Ruben. "I hope everybody has good brakes. I don't like being wedged in between two big vehicles when we're going downhill."

The traffic moved slowly down the long hill. Mr. Ruben tried to keep his distance from the truck in front of him.

"The camper is almost into our back seat!" shouted Frayda. "Can't we move a little faster?"

"I'm already on top of the truck and I can't pass him here," said Mr. Ruben.

He was a little worried. The diesel truck in front was going too slow and the camper in back was going to fast. From the rear-view mirror, he felt as if he could almost touch the driver.

"Daddy, I'm scared," called Chani. "They look like they're going to crash into us."

"Well, let's hope they won't—I can't go any faster."

Now they were going uphill and their worries were reversed. It seemed as though the diesel might slide down onto their car!

"Pass him, Daddy. Get in front of him," suggested Frayda.

"I can't. It's a no-passing zone. And I can't see what's coming from the other direction. On a two-lane highway, it's too dangerous to pass a large vehicle like that."

The roller coaster ride continued; first up, then down, their small car always in between the huge truck and the large camper. Up and down—always much too close to the truck in the front or the camper in the back. It was quiet in the car. Mr. Ruben felt a tight gnawing in his stomach as he clutched the wheel.

Frayda stopped waving to the children in the camper. She was angry that they were driving almost on top of her.

To their great relief, the road flattened out after the next hill. But as Mr. Ruben tried to pass the diesel, the truck speeded up. He couldn't understand why. So he slowed down, hoping the camper would want to get in front of him, but it stayed right in place.

"What's going on? I can't get out of here," he mumbled, very frustrated.

They continued in a line, until the highway broadened into four lanes. Mr. Ruben sped off in front of the diesel, much to everyone's relief, but within moments, the children's grumbling began again.

"Ma, I'm really uncomfortable," said Frayda. "Couldn't we pull over to the side and trade places?"

"Just hold on a few minutes, dear."

"Daddy, look, our gas gauge is on empty!" exclaimed Chani.

"It's always on empty," answered Mr. Ruben.

"How is that possible?"

"Because it doesn't work."

"Then how do you know when you're out of gas?"

"Because I fill the tank up every hundred and fifty miles."

"Is that safe? Couldn't you make a mistake?" asked Chani, alarmed.

"I could, but I try to be careful. Have we been stranded yet?"

"Please stop for a minute and let me trade places," begged Frayda. "My legs feel numb already."

"Then we can fill up on gas, too," said Chani. "There's a station in front of us. I want to make sure we have enough."

"No, we're not stopping. It's another twelve miles and I think we ought to be able to make it just fine."

Frayda's moans and groans were heard from the rear seat as they passed the station.

A few moments later, Frayda asked, "Why are we slowing up, Dad?"

"There's something wrong with the car."

"What's wrong?" asked Mrs. Ruben.

"The gas pedal is down to the floor but nothing is happening. We're slowing down."

"Oh, no!"

Frightened, the children began to cry, "What will we do?"

"We're stuck. Oh, no!"

"Mummy, I'm scared."

"I told you to fill up on gas, Daddy."

Mr. Ruben steered the car off the road to a stop along the guard rail.

"Sol, this isn't a good place to stop. We're on a bridge."

"There's nothing we can do about that, Liba. The car stopped."

"What now?" sobbed Chani.

"Should we hitch a ride to get some help?" asked Fradya.

"Not we, but I," answered their father.

"Daddy, you can't leave us here alone on the bridge. It's almost nighttime," said Chani.

"I'll take care of you, baby," teased Frayda.

"Stop calling me 'baby'!"

"Look, children," said Mrs. Ruben, "this is no time for fighting. We'll have to decide what the most sensible thing to do is, and *Hashem* will help. Now, everyone be quiet and Daddy will decide what is best."

As they were speaking, the trailer which had been following them for so long pulled to a stop in front of their car. A middle-aged man, wearing a baseball cap and glasses, emerged from the cab of the camper and walked over to their car.

"Having some trouble here?" he asked. "Can I help?"

He and Mr. Ruben opened the hood and spoke for a few minutes. Then the man returned to his trailer. Mr. Ruben closed the hood with a resounding slam, wiped his forehead with a handkerchief and walked over to his wife.

"Liba, I guess I misjudged. We are probably out of gas. These people are willing to drive me to the nearest exit to get some. Hand me the empty can in the back, please."

"OK, everybody out to the trailer," shouted Chani.

"Hold on a minute," said Mr. Ruben, "everybody stays here but me."

A chorus of outrage poured from the back seat.

"Why?"

"We can't stay here alone."

"I'm scared."

"It's getting dark."

"Daddy, you can't leave us."

"I want to go home."

"Quiet, everyone, and listen. Number one, we can't just pick up and leave the car and all of our belongings alone on the road, because in all likelihood they won't be here when we get back. Number two, it's eight miles to the next exit and if I can't get a lift back, it's too far for everyone to walk. Stay *in* the car, *lock* the doors, and if anyone stops, close the windows. As soon as I get to a station, I'll notify the highway patrol. I'll try to get back as soon as I can." And Mr. Ruben, can in hand, climbed into the waiting trailer.

Liba silently said a quick prayer for her husband's safe return and for their own welfare. She didn't like being left here alone with the children. She didn't like her husband going off with strangers. She didn't like being on the edge of a viaduct. She didn't like the fact that it would soon be night. She didn't like anything at all about their situation — not one bit! Nevertheless, she reassured the children.

"Listen, children, we're on our way to perform several *mitzvos*. One big *mitzva* is *kibbud av va'em*. Do you realize how happy we will make Bubby and Zeidy when they see us? Secondly, we have *shaliach mitzva* money — money we are bringing for *tzedaka*. And people who are messengers for *mitzvos* are under *Hashem*'s special protection. By the way, it just occurred to me that we haven't said *tefillas haderech* today! Maybe that's why we're in this mess now! Frayda, take out your *siddur*."

The sun was beginning to set, and the low western rays shone directly through the windows of the hot car. They were all tired, cranky and frightened. No one spoke.

An enormous trailer truck swept by them at full speed. The crowded car seemed to tremble. Daniel, afraid that they would topple over the edge of the bridge, screamed and climbed over the seat to bury his head in his mother's lap. Mrs. Ruben stroked his head.

"Now, now, everything will be all right. *Hashem* is watching over us, and He'll take care of us. Don't be afraid. Frayda, did you find the place in your *siddur* yet?"

"Yes."

"Fine. Then everyone listen. Go ahead, Frayda."

Frayda recited the *tefilla* and, except for Daniel, everyone felt a little better. He continued to sob, and each time a trailer truck came by, which was rather often, he began to cry.

Minutes seemed like hours, and there was no sign of Mr. Ruben. Even Frayda's show of bravery began to waver. Mrs. Ruben encouraged them to sing, but the half-hearted songs soon dwindled to a stop.

It was hot — very hot. And dark. A thick, black darkness. Suddenly, Mrs. Ruben realized that their parked car could not be seen!

She didn't drive, but she knew there were emergency lights in the car. She began to examine the dashboard, pushing and pulling knobs to see what would happen.

"What are you doing?" asked Frayda.

"Trying to find the button for those flashing lights, the ones for an emergency."

"Oh, here," said Frayda as she leaned over and flicked them on. "Good you thought of it."

"It's strange that I thought of it. I hardly know anything about the car, but you see, *Hashem* is taking care of us."

Mrs. Ruben looked at her watch again. Her husband had been away a long time. Suddenly the sky lit up with a three-pronged flash. Peals of thunder rolled through the air, and then the rain began. Sheets of water covered the windshield, and before long, they could see nothing at all.

Frayda sat in the back saying *tehillim* aloud. Daniel had fallen asleep in his mother's lap, while Chani sat silently gazing into the storm.

A loud bang on the side of the car made everyone jump. They peered out the windows but couldn't see who or what it was. Chani started saying *Shema* out loud. Moments later a flashlight shone through the window of the car.

"Open up!" said a strange face at the window.

"Keep the doors closed!" cried Mrs. Ruben.

Again a pounding on the doors and the flashlight through the window.

"Open up! Open up!"

"Keep the doors shut," repeated the frightened Mrs. Ruben.

"Highway patrol, lady!"

"I don't know if they are or not. Keep the doors shut," she said again.

Another face on the other side of the car. It was pouring too hard to see it clearly. Then, a third face by the back window. The third face moved to the front of the car.

Terror gripped the stranded passengers. Again, a pounding on the door.

"Liba, open up! It's me, Sol!"

"Oh, *baruch Hashem*," said Mrs. Ruben, in relief, as she recognized her husband's voice.

When she reached over and unlocked the door, Mr. Ruben sloshed onto the seat.

"Thank you. Thank you again. I really appreciate it," he hollered out into the rain.

"Glad to be of help," came a voice from the downpour. "I'll follow you awhile."

"Thanks."

"I hope I got that gas cap back on the tank right. It's hard to see in the rain, even with a flashlight," Mr. Ruben mumbled.

"Oh, so that's what that loud noise was," exclaimed his wife. "It really scared us!"

Mr. Ruben started the motor, and the car slowly left the viaduct and proceeded down the slippery road.

The family was ecstatic that their father was back safe and sound, and they listened eagerly to every detail of his adventure.

"I was riding in the trailer with the Maxwells, the family who stopped to help us. They were about to turn off the exit when there was a loud 'pop' and they swerved off the main road onto the ramp with a flat tire. It was the second flat they had had in twenty miles, and they were traveling on their spare. That's why they were going so slowly. Anyway, I got out and told them that I would walk to the nearest service station and would send help back to them.

"When I got to the gas station, I notified the highway patrol that we were stuck on the viaduct. Then I told the station manager about the Maxwells. He said he would get someone to them as soon as he could spare a man. They were very busy at the time. At first I decided to wait for the man to drive down to the Maxwells so that I would have less to walk. But when it started to get dark and it looked like rain, I was worried about you, so I decided to take the gas can and start walking.

"As I was partway down the road, a diesel truck pulled up from the opposite direction. The driver honked and yelled out the window to ask me what was wrong. You won't believe this, but it was the same truck that had been in front of us going down those hills. He had pulled off the highway to take a short nap. When I told him that we had run out of gas, he said he'd drive me back to my car if I would wait for him to grab a sandwich. It would have taken me longer to walk, so I waited and I got here at the same time the highway patrol did."

"So you see," continued Mrs. Ruben, "both the camper and the diesel truck were a great help. After we spent such a long time complaining about them, it turns out that we have to be very thankful that they were there! *Hashem* always knows what He's doing, even if we don't always understand; and whatever He does has a purpose!"

In grateful silence, the Rubens continued on their way to Seattle.

❋ A Perfect Blue Plush Chanuka

❋ Elisheva sat curled up in the corner of the heavy brown mohair sofa, absorbed, as usual, in the Sears catalogue. As usual, she was looking at the coat section, particularly the navy-blue plush coat with the matching belt. Her gray eyes lingered over the page as her small finger-tips lovingly caressed the picture over and over again.

It seemed to Mrs. Markovitz that her eleven-year-old daughter had been longing for that coat forever. It broke her heart to watch Elisheva, night after night, pining away for that coat. A tear trickled down her cheek, falling into the pan of potatoes she was peeling. She had long since given up trying to divert Elisheva's attention from the catalogue. All her efforts had been futile. Every night mother and daughter sat together silently in the two-room attic apartment, each engrossed in her own solitary thoughts and dreams.

Mrs. Markowitz worried about the effects of the past two years on her daughter. Elisheva had friends,

and her school work was fine, but the evenings, the long silent evenings with the catalogue, frightened her. She thought about the groove the child had worn into the corner of the couch. She thought about the sad, far-away look in Elisheva's eyes. She thought about the unfortunate turn of events in their lives. She thought about her husband, Meyer, and the boys — Yitzy, Shlomo and Yehuda. She thought about how much she wished she could get Elisheva that coat, and she sighed a long, weary sigh.

But sighing didn't help, and there were things to be done. Mrs. Markowitz pulled out the frying pan, heated the oil and began to fry the potatoes. She cut up carrots and celery, and put three eggs on the stove to boil. Slices of two-day-old bread and milk completed the sparse but healthy meal. Considering her weekly take-home pay, she was happy to serve nutritious meals, even though they did eat a lot of potatoes.

"Supper's almost ready, Shevala. Go wash up."

Elisheva nodded absentmindedly and returned to her fantasy. It was always the same dream — the face of the girl in the catalogue wearing the navy-blue plush coat would melt away and Elisheva's face would be there instead. She would then lift herself out of the catalogue and walk grandly around the room, modeling her very own new, blue plush coat. Then she would walk right down the stairs and out the door. Everyone would turn and look at the beautiful coat. She would walk straight down Phillips Avenue all the way to the yeshiva and through the front door. Her classmates would ooh and aah as they stroked the soft velvety material.

"*Tischadshi*, Sheva," they would say. "It's just gorgeous! How beautiful, Sheva! Wear it in the best of health . . ."

"Shevala, come on, honey, it will get cold. Let's eat."

Elisheva was startled by her mother's voice. She got up slowly and went into the kitchen to wash for supper.

"We got a letter from the boys today. They did well in their *bechinos* this semester. It's snowing very hard in New York, but Yehuda said his friend Tuvya might rent a car. If he does, he and Yehuda will drive in for Chanuka vacation. Wouldn't it be nice to have at least one of your brothers home for Chanuka, Sheva?"

"Do you really think Yehuda might come?" asked Sheva. "We haven't seen any of them since last Pesach."

Mrs. Markowitz's heart melted as she saw Elisheva come alive for the first time in weeks. She held her pigtailed daughter close.

"Let me see the letter, Mama. Where is it?"

Mrs. Markowitz reached into her apron pocket and produced the folded letter. She watched the smile spread across her daughter's face, and she prayed that Tuvya would rent the car, for Elisheva's sake.

Supper was happy that night. Elisheva rambled on and on about what they would do if Yehuda came home. She skipped about the kitchen, helped dry the dishes, and chattered merrily as they opened the hide-a-bed couch and prepared for sleep.

"It's good to see your children happy," thought Mrs. Markowitz. "It seems so long since anyone of us has been happy . . ."

Her thoughts went back over the past two years. She remembered the pleasant home they had had on Hobart Street; the sounds of children on the stairs; the beautiful Shabbosos with family and friends. And then . . . then Meyer, her husband, suddenly became ill.

"Tuberculosis," the doctors said. "But how? In this day and age? It's 1960! People don't get tuberculosis anymore."

Reb Meyer had been the *mashgiach*, the supervisor for *kashruth*, at Mount Sinai Hospital for nineteen years. Someone working with the food had been a carrier, and somehow Reb Meyer, while in the kitchen, had contracted the disease. She remembered the scandal at the hospital, but most of all she remembered the trauma at home.

"Reb Meyer must go to a sanitarium or a convalescent home . . . the disease is contagious and it takes a long time to recover," said Dr. Kravitz. "He has some other complications as well."

They had some money in the bank, but not nearly enough . . . not nearly enough. No money was coming in, but large sums were going out for food, household bills, clothing, every-day expenses. The medical bills were the worst of all. The insurance paid something, but it was a nightmare. Mrs. Markowitz had never worked outside her home, and she had no marketable skills. The community offered to help, but she and her husband had never accepted charity, and they didn't want to start now.

Fifteen-year-old Shlomo and seventeen-year-old

Yehuda were learning in a yeshiva in New York. Yitzy had become bar mitzva just before his father became ill, and it was decided that he would join his brother in New York. Mrs. Markowitz found a job working the cash register at Berkowitz's Fish Market on Fourth Avenue, but it wasn't enough to support her family, so eventually, she decided to sell the house and rent a small apartment for herself and Elisheva.

Except for the day they discovered her husband's illness, that was the saddest day of her life. That lovely, lovely house with its ringing laughter and beautiful children was no longer theirs. And it was the breaking point for Elisheva, too. Weeks and weeks of sleepless nights plagued the tear-filled child and her mother. It was difficult for them to comfort one another.

As the weeks and months went by, there was some encouragement from the doctors and Mrs. Markowitz's worries were lightened. Elisheva, however, was so young that to her it seemed a lifetime since her father had been home. At times she wondered if he would ever come back. Her brothers never came home either, because there was no money for trainfare. Even home wasn't home . . . it was the Schwartzes' attic.

But what saddened little Elisheva most often was her brown coat. It looked more like a jacket than a coat. The sleeves were so short that she wore long gloves to cover her exposed arms. She felt miserable on the playground and ashamed when she saw everyone else in their new coats.

Mrs. Markowitz was also unhappy. "But *Hashem* will help us—I'm sure He will," she thought. "And

perhaps with His help, Yehuda will be home soon too."
She smiled at the thought of seeing her eldest son
again.

The next morning it rained. Heavy pellets of water
struck the roof and windowpane with no relief in sight.
Elisheva took her schoolbag and umbrella from the
closet, lifted the latch on the door, and ran down the
stairs.

"Hi, Mrs. Schwartz," she called out as she rounded
the stairs to the first-floor landing. "Guess what?
Yehuda's coming home for Chanuka!"

Mrs. Schwartz pulled her blue robe closer, around
the neck as Sheva opened the door.

"Really? I'm so happy for you, my dear, and for
your mother too! Put your umbrella up. It's really
coming down out there."

Sheva left the house and opened the umbrella. As
she rounded the corner, she caught sight of the
Handleman twins. She doubled back quickly before
they saw her and took the longer route to school to
avoid them. Now she would have to go down Murray
Avenue, and it would take her ten minutes extra to get
to school. But it was better, she decided, to get
drenched in the rain than to be badgered by the twins.

The Handleman boys weren't really *bad*, just
terribly annoying. They were practical jokers and
teasers who thought they were very funny at other
people's expense. They teased Sheva about her small
coat relentlessly, making wisecracks whenever they
saw her. That was one of the reasons she so desperately
wished she had a new coat.

She hurried on in the rain and waited at the corner for the light to change. As Elisheva stepped into the street, she kicked something. Looking down, she saw a black glass-case on the ground. She stooped to pick it up and found a pair of thick glasses inside the case. As Sheva searched for a name, she heard a car honking. "Hey, little girl, better watch yourself in the street!" Sheva shoved the case into her pocket and quickly crossed the street.

In her hurry to get to school on time, she began to run. At the bottom of Beacon Street, the water had collected in a large stream. Sheva tried to jump across, but she landed right in the middle of the muddy stream, the water right up to her ankles.

"Oy," she cried aloud, "I hope I don't get sick!"

At school, Mrs. Melofsky immediately took Elisheva down to the kitchen and helped her dry herself near the oven. Her shoes were soaking wet, but one of the girls lent her a pair of tennis shoes which were in her locker.

"Bring me Sheva's coat, Devora," called Mrs. Melofsky. "We'll hang it here by the oven to dry out. The whole bottom is wet. And just look at your skirt, Elisheva. What did you do? Sit down in a puddle?"

"Almost," laughed Elisheva as she described the river on Beacon Street.

Mrs. Melofsky returned to class, leaving Devora to help Elisheva. As Devora reached for the coat, the forgotten glass-case fell to the floor.

"I didn't know you wear glasses, Sheva," said Devora.

"I don't. I found them in the street on my way to school today. I want to find out whose they are."

"Where did you find them?"

"On Murray Avenue."

"On Murray Avenue? There are about fifty doctors' offices over there. How will you ever find out where these glasses came from? There's no name on the case.

"Look," said Devora as she held up the spectacles, "they're awfully funny-looking glasses. They're so big and thick, especially this round part in the middle. I bet whomever they belong to must need them badly, but I don't see how you're going to find the owner. Unless you put an ad in the paper. But anyone who needs such thick glasses probably has more than one pair. I wouldn't worry about it if I were you. Come on, let's go. Mrs. Melofsky will think we went home."

But Elisheva *did* worry. All morning long she thought about putting an ad in the paper, but she knew she couldn't do that. It would cost too much money. What could she do for the person who had lost the glasses?

Recess time arrived. The rain had stopped and many of the children, ignoring the puddles, ran out to the playground. Sheva and Devora found a quiet corner of the lunchroom and settled down to play jacks. Suddenly they were pelted by wads of paper, rubber bands and small pieces of chalk. The whooping laughter they heard left no doubt in their minds as to who the culprits were—the Handleman twins.

"Sammy and Abie, you'd better get out of here, or I'll report you to Rabbi Perloff," shouted Sheva.

"You do that and next time you won't jump into the puddle — we'll push you in," retorted Abie.

"Yeh, all the way up to your coat! Your short, short coat," laughed Sammy.

"Leave her alone and get out of here," said Devora authoritatively. After a few more pieces of flying chalk, the twins finally left.

"Don't pay any attention to them, Sheva, they're crude. Somebody needs to give them a lesson in manners."

"I just can't stand it anymore, Devora. They're always making fun of me. I can't help it if this is the only coat I have. I would tell Rabbi Perloff about them, but then it would become a big thing and my mother would get upset. I went down Murray Avenue just to get away from them this morning, but they saw me anyway. They are just so . . . so nasty!" She struggled to hold back the tears.

Devora patted her friend on the shoulder and said, "Come on, let's forget about them and finish our game. Do you want to come over after school and bake cookies?"

"I don't think so. I'd really like to find out whom the glasses belong to."

"Oh, Sheva, how are you going to do that?"

"I don't know. Not yet anyway."

That evening, while waiting for her mother to come home, Elisheva took out the glass-case and searched for some clue as to the owner's identity. When she opened the frames she noticed the tiny initials engraved into the right temple — B.G.

"Those must be the initials of the person who owns them," she said excitedly.

"Who owns what?" asked her mother as she opened the door.

Elisheva ran to kiss her mother. "Look," she said, "this morning on the way to school I found these glasses, and I want to give them back because the person must need them very badly because they're so thick and I couldn't figure out who they belonged to and I felt so bad and now I found the initials on the inside of the frame so I can give them back and . . ."

"Wait a minute, wait a minute, slow down," laughed her mother. "I didn't hear a word you said. Let me put these groceries down, and then you can start all over again."

Sheva slowly recounted the events of the day, ending with the discovery of the initials.

"What you really need to do is put an ad in the paper, but we don't have the money."

"I know," answered Sheva sadly.

That night as she lay on the couch, Sheva was unable to sleep. Someone needed those glasses, and she tossed and turned trying to find a solution. Finally, she shoved the pillow up against the back of the couch and sat up, curling her arms around her legs and resting her chin on her knees. She thought very hard until she hit upon a plan. "I am going to go to every eye doctor's office on Murray Avenue and ask if they have a patient with the intials B.G. I'll find the person. Pittsburgh is a big city, but I just know I can find the owner. It's really too bad we don't have a phone. That would make things a lot easier. Maybe I could ask Mrs. Schwartz. No, I'll just go there after school tomorrow."

Satisfied with her plan of action, she slid back under the covers and was soon fast asleep.

The next day moved slowly for Elisheva, who was anxious to start on her mission. At last it was four o'clock and school was over. She had exactly one hour before everything closed. Hurrying to put her things away, she decided to start at the Lark Building. It was the smallest. Maybe she could make the rounds of all the eye doctors in an hour.

Elisheva stepped timidly into the cool, dark entry-way of the Lark Building. She looked up at the directory on the wall and made a mental list of all the eye doctors in the building . . . one on the first floor, three on the second and five on the fourth . . . nine offices in all.

Elisheva walked up to the first floor to Dr. Hammer's office. She opened the door cautiously and found the waiting room full of patients. A little frightened, she approached the nurse at the desk.

"Do you have an appointment?"

"No. I found these glasses out on the street, and I was wondering if they belong to any of your patients."

Sheva handed the case to the nurse, who opened it and examined the glasses.

"These are special glasses for people who have had a certain type of eye operation," said the nurse. "We don't do that here. You would need to find a specialist. Try Dr. Johnson on the fourth floor."

Thanking the nurse, Sheva took the glasses and

hurried to the fourth floor. She found the office and walked up to the receptionist.

"Do you have an appointment? Is your mother with you?"

"No," explained Elisheva. "I'm trying to find the owner of these glasses that I found in the street."

The receptionist looked at the glasses. "No name? We have over one hundred patients wearing glasses like these."

"They have initials on the frames—B.G. Maybe someone in your files has these initials. Could you look?"

The receptionist went back to the files and looked under "G." "Sorry, dear," she said when she came back a few minutes later, "nobody with B.G. Why don't you try Dr. Burns down the hall?"

Sheva went to Dr. Burns's office, but she had no luck there either.

"Maybe Devora is right," she thought, "I'll probably never find the owner." But something made Sheva continue her search until she had gone to every office in the building. With no luck. Four afternoons in a row, Sheva went from building to building, from office to office, and it was always the same story—no one with the initials B.G.

On *erev Shabbos*, Sheva went straight home. There was no time to look for the mysterious owner. In the winter, Shabbos began early, and Sheva had to help with the Shabbos preparations. Mrs. Markowitz finished work at two o'clock, which didn't leave much time for her to prepare for Shabbos.

Sheva cut the vegetables and left them soaking in cold water in the big pan. Then she set the table and began to polish the candlesticks. Suddenly she heard footsteps running up the stairs, and Devora shouting her name excitedly. Sheva ran to answer the door.

"What is it?" cried Sheva.

"You'll never guess what happened. Just guess. Go ahead! No, you'll never guess. Well, go ahead, guess. No, I'll tell you!"

"Well, make up your mind, Devora."

"My mother was taking a coffee break this afternoon, and she happened to glance at the newspaper on the table, and look what she saw in the Lost and Found section!" Devora shoved the newspaper under Sheva's nose.

Lost: Vicinity Forbes & Murray Avenues
Black glass-case & glasses
Reward   5382 Shady Lane

"That's my glass-case!" shouted Sheva. "As soon as my mother comes home, I'll go right over. Want to come with me, Devora?"

"Sure! That number is all the way down near Fifth Avenue. It's probably near that big spooky house on the corner. Maybe it *is* the spooky house on the corner! What will we do then?"

"Then we'll get to see the inside," said Elisheva, opening her eyes wide in anticipation.

When Mrs. Markowitz arrived home, she gave Elisheva permission to go, providing she promised to be back half-an-hour before candle-lighting time. Promising not to dawdle on the way, the two girls rushed out.

Half walking, half running, they hurried to Shady Lane. As they searched for the correct number, they came closer and closer to Fifth Avenue. Devora was ready to go home as they neared the scary house, but Elisheva dragged her along. To their great relief, the girls found the proper address two doors away from the corner. They saw a green-shuttered mansion covered with ivy. A towering oak tree shaded the entire front of the house.

"Wow!" exclaimed Devora. "This is some house. No wonder they're giving a reward."

"It's funny," said Elisheva thoughtfully. "Do you know how many times I've been down this street, and I never really noticed any of the houses except the spooky one on the corner. What a beautiful, beautiful house this is."

The two young girls walked up to the front door, and Elisheva rang the bell. A few moments later they heard footsteps and a tall, thin boy opened the door.

"Hello. Can I help you?" he asked.

The girls stood awkwardly for a minute and then Elisheva spoke up.

"Is this the house that put the ad in the paper about the glasses?"

"Yes, it is," answered the boy.

"Well, I found the glasses. I have them in my pocket."

"Oh, wonderful," exclaimed the boy, grinning from ear to ear. "Come in! Grandma will be so happy. Come in, come in."

The girls entered a large hall with marble floors and huge paintings hanging on the walls.

"Just a minute," said the boy, "I'll find out if Grandma can see you now."

He raced up an enormous staircase shouting, "Grandma, Grandma . . ."

Elisheva and Devora immediately began whispering to each other.

"Did you ever see such a gorgeous house?"

"It looks like the museum," said Elisheva.

"Boy, I bet you'll get a great reward, Sheva."

"I don't care about the reward. I just want to give the glasses back."

Presently the boy returned.

"Come on up," he said. "Grandma is awake."

They were ushered into a large room. An old lady with dark glasses was sitting on a couch opposite a fireplace.

"Hello. Are you the girls who found my glasses? How wonderful! May I have them?"

"What's your name, ma'am?" asked Sheva. "These glasses have initials on them."

"I know," the old lady said. "B.G. — in the right temple. That stands for Bernice Goodman."

"That's right," cried Sheva. "They *are* yours!" She handed the case to the woman, who put them on.

"Oh, thank goodness! I can see again! Now, let me see the lovely child who found my glasses." She took Sheva by the hand and planted a gentle kiss on her forehead.

"My dear, you have no idea how you have helped an

old woman. I had a very serious operation on my eyes, and I must have these special glasses. Now you will have your reward for returning them to me. Charles, where is my checkbook?"

"Oh, no, Mrs. Goodman, that won't be necessary," said Sheva. "My reward is knowing you have your glasses and can see again."

"But I offered a reward, and you will get one!" insisted Mrs. Goodman.

"No, no," cried Sheva. "I'm glad you have your glasses. I have to hurry now. I promised my mother I'd be right back."

Sheva quickly walked toward the door, but Devora grasped her arm and whispered loudly, "Sheva, now you can get your coat . . ." Suddenly she felt Sheva's elbow poking her in the ribs.

"Shh . . . ," whispered Sheva. "Good-bye," she said in a loud voice.

"I don't even know your name," called Mrs. Goodman. But Sheva was already halfway down the stairs. She hurried out the front door with Devora running after her and protesting.

"You're crazy! You could have had money for a new coat!"

"I told you I didn't want a reward. I wanted the *mitzva* of returning the lost glasses." The two girls hurried home, arguing all the way.

Shabbos came and went. One day followed another as Chanuka came nearer, and Sheva grew more and more excited at the prospect of seeing her brother again.

Early one December morning Sheva awoke to find the world blanketed with the first deep snow of the season. The snowflakes whirled about the attic window, and she could barely see the street below. Her mother had left her a steaming pan of oatmeal on the stove and a note instructing her to wear her heavy cardigan sweater.

After eating, Sheva put on the bulky blue cardigan and her coat. The coat seemed to grow smaller and smaller each time she wore it, but with the sweater underneath, she found that she couldn't even button it. The sweater sleeves were so thick that she couldn't pull them through the coat sleeves, and the result was that she had two bulky bulges at her elbows. Tears came to her eyes, and she fervently prayed that the Handleman boys wouldn't bother her.

The day, however, was quiet, and in the afternoon when Sheva returned from school, all she wanted to do was curl up on the couch with some hot cocoa. It had been a long, hard day with three tests. And there was still a lot of homework to do. Maybe she would just look through the catalogue for a while before doing her homework. She hoped that they would have some meat for supper. It had been a long time since they last had any. "Meatloaf would be good," she thought, "and some nice thick vegetable soup."

As she climbed the stairs to the attic, she saw the large box from Levy's Department Store lying outside their door. On the front of the package was a sticker with her name. Elisheva was so excited that she ripped off the wrapping even before entering her apartment.

"Oh my! Oh my! Oh . . ." was all she could say.
There in the package lay a coat, almost exactly like the
one in the catalogue—blue and plush, soft and lovely,
but with a red belt instead of a blue one. Her fingers
stroked it as she hugged it to her body. She laughed
and cried all at once. Then she noticed the card.

> Dear Elisheva,
>
> Your friend Devora was kind enough to tell me
> all about the coat. A dear, good girl like you
> certainly deserves it. And you can't give it back
> because it was on Final Sale, and I certainly can't
> wear it. Now use it in the best of health. I do hope
> you will come to visit me. Have a Happy
> Chanuka!
>
> Love,
> Mrs. Goodman

Elisheva's heart was beating like a drum as she put
the coat on and rushed to the mirror. She turned round
and round, to see it from every angle.

"Hello, Shevala," called Mrs. Markowitz as she
came into the house. "Mr. Berkowitz let me off early
because of the weather, and guess what? I bought some
chopped meat on the way home. It's a good day to have
a nice, hot meatloaf . . ." her voice trailed off as she
came into the room. "Sheva, what are you wearing?"

Sheva handed her mother the card. After reading
the note, Mrs. Markowitz took her daughter in her
arms.

"It's a beautiful coat," she said, her voice trembling, "a beautiful coat. You see, Shevala, *Hashem* has many ways of providing!"

The next morning Elisheva donned her new coat and set off happily for school. She took the direct route this morning, not worrying whether or not she would meet the Handleman twins. And she did meet them. They looked at her and stared. They whispered to each other. And they walked right past her without saying a word.

"Good!" she thought.

At school that morning, Elisheva's dream came true. All the girls stood around admiring the lovely coat, and happiest of all was her friend Devora. Elisheva called Devora aside and said, "You shouldn't have told her, Devora."

"I know," smiled Devora. "But I wanted you to have the coat." When the bell rang, the girls hung their coats in the lockers and went to class.

Later that afternoon Devora was called into the office for a telephone call from home. On her way back to her room, she saw Sam and Abie, the Handleman twins, hurrying out of the girls' locker room. They disappeared into the boys section of the building.

"Hmm, wonder what they're up to?" thought Devora. "I bet they took our mascot again."

The girls had an oversized orange bear which had been given to them by a former classmate. It now served as mascot of the locker room and sat in a place of honor on top of the largest row of lockers. Sometimes it was missing. Then, somehow, it would pop up again in a day or two. The girls always suspected the Handleman boys, but now she might have proof. Devora hurried into the locker room, but there was Mumfi, safe and sound in his proper place.

"Oh, well," thought Devora, "maybe they just went to get a drink from the fountain. I shouldn't be so suspicious." She returned to class.

Before school ended, Mrs. Melofsky asked Devora to stay a few minutes longer to discuss a new project.

"Wait for me, Sheva. I'll walk you halfway home."

"OK," she answered, "I'll meet you at the lockers."

Five minutes later, Devora came into the locker room. A group of girls was standing around Elisheva who was crying.

"What's wrong? What happened?" asked Devora as she pushed her way into the crowd. "Oh!" cried Devora, as her eyes widened in disbelief. "How did that happen?"

There stood Elisheva, her best friend, in the brand-new blue coat—but it wasn't blue anymore. It had been streaked with white chalk marks from one end to the other. The girls had tried to wipe it off, but the chalk had only smeared and spread, making it look even worse. Sheva's face was as white as the chalk marks. Her lips were quivering as she ran to her best friend and buried her head in Devora's shoulder.

"Oh, Devora, my new coat! My beautiful new coat! Who could do such an awful thing?"

Devora put her arms around Sheva. "I just thought of something, Sheva. Come on, we're going to Rabbi Perloff's office. He has to see this."

Devora and Elisheva walked to the principal's office.

"Mrs. Horowitz," said Devora to the secretary, "we have to see Rabbi Perloff right away."

"Why, Elisheva, what happened to your coat?" asked Mrs. Horowitz as she looked up from her desk.

"That's what we have to see Rabbi Perloff about!"

"Just a minute and let me see if he's busy."

Mrs. Horowitz walked to Rabbi Perloff's office. She knocked gently and opened the door.

"Rabbi Perloff, there are two young ladies here whom I think you ought to see right away."

Rabbi Perloff, tall and thin, with a heavy black beard, came to the door and invited the girls in.

"Elisheva, what happened to your coat?"

Sheva tried to hold back her tears, but when she tried to speak, only a sob came out.

"I'll tell you what happened, Rabbi Perloff," said Devora. "Sheva just got this beautiful new coat yesterday, and this is the first time she's worn it. When she went to her locker, she found it all chalked up like this, and I'm almost positive I know who did it."

"You are? How is that? Did you see someone actually do it?"

"No, but this afternoon Mrs. Horowitz called me to the phone and on the way back to class, I saw Abie and Sammy Handleman leaving the girls' locker room. I thought they went in to take Mumfi, so I went to check. But Mumfi was in his regular place, so I figured maybe they just went to get a drink. I never dreamed they'd do such a terrible thing. I just know they did it, Rabbi Perloff."

"One should never accuse others without proof, Devora."

"But, Rabbi Perloff, they tease people all the time and play practical jokes. They probably think they're very funny. They were always teasing Sheva about her old coat. I told her to complain a long time ago, but she wouldn't."

"Well, I shall certainly look into the matter immediately. Now, Sheva, in the meantime, I want you to have your coat cleaned, but not until *after school tomorrow*. And have the bill sent to the school. We'll take care of it. Now try to smile. I know it's hard, but your coat will be as good as new by the time your . . ." Rabbi Perloff paused and hesitated, "by the time your brother gets home for Chanuka."

The next morning at nine o'clock sharp, Rabbi Perloff sent for the Handleman boys. The two red-haired youngsters walked hesitantly into the office. Rabbi Perloff sat silently behind his large desk, stroking his beard and nodding his head. He didn't speak for a long time. He just sat there stroking his beard and staring at the twins who began to squirm and fidget uncomfortably. Finally, he stood up from behind the desk and walked over to the boys. He began pacing back and forth in front of them, his hands clasped behind his back. Suddenly, his towering figure stopped directly in front of Abie and Sammy. Then, in a very matter-of-fact tone, he asked, "So, tell me, what's new, boys?"

The twins, already frightened, were taken aback. Neither could think of an answer to such an unexpected question.

When they remained silent, Rabbi Perloff continued, "I hear you've been busy with a new project. Tell me about it."

"New project? What new project?" asked Abie.

"Why, I hear that you've gone into fashion design. Is this true?"

"F . . . fashion design?" stammered Sammy.

"Why yes, " said Rabbi Perloff as he walked to the office door. He opened it wide and ushered in Sheva, wearing her chalk-marked coat. "I believe this is an original creation of yours."

Abie's face turned almost as red as his hair, and Sammy lowered his eyes and stared at the green carpet on the floor. Guilt covered their faces.

"We were just having some fun. We didn't really hurt anyone," muttered Sammy, still staring at the floor.

"You didn't?" answered Rabbi Perloff. "Don't you think that hurting someone's feelings is 'hurting'? Don't you think vandalizing and destroying property is hurting? Fun is *not fun* when it is at the expense of another person. What you have done is very cruel. Obviously, you are not learning the things we teach you in class, or you couldn't possibly display such poor *middos*. I've tolerated your minor pranks, but now you've gone too far. It's about time you boys were taught a lesson.

"First of all, you will pay to have Elisheva's coat cleaned. Secondly, your parents are going to be notified that unless your behavior changes quite a bit, you will be expelled from school. And last, and probably most important, your punishment will fit the crime. Instead of spending so much time dreaming up nasty pranks, you are going to spend time thinking of ways to do something good. As of now, you two are officially the heads of a new club which will be called the *Ahavas Chesed* Club, and you will initiate a school membership drive. You will think of at least two good deeds to do every week. Every Friday afternoon, I want a report from you. Is that understood? Maybe by the time school is out, you will have learned to use your energy and your bright ideas for something constructive!

"Last of all," continued Rabbi Perloff, "you will both apologize to Elisheva for damaging her coat and for causing her so much anguish!"

Abie and Sammy mumbled an apology and went sheepishly back to class. Elisheva hung her coat in the locker room while Rabbi Perloff made a phone call to Mrs. Handleman. When school was over, Sheva took the coat to the cleaners.

The days flew by. Soon it would be Chanuka, and each evening Sheva marked off a day on the calendar, until there were only three days left. Yesterday they had received a letter saying that Yehuda would arrive sometime Wednesday afternoon.

Elisheva took down the *menora*, polished it, and wrapped it up again so that it wouldn't tarnish. Then Mrs. Markowitz and Elisheva baked and baked—all kinds of cakes and dozens of cookies. Mrs. Markowitz was happier than Sheva had ever remembered seeing her. Her face glowed.

Wednesday morning finally arrived, and Chanuka vacation had started. Elisheva quivered with anticipation, walking back and forth through the tiny apartment, making sure that everything was in perfect shape. Even though she knew it was hours before her brother would arrive, she kept looking out the window as if she could hurry his coming. Mrs. Markowitz had to work all day, so the meal and the *latkes* and just about everything had been prepared the night before.

In the afternoon, Devora came over to help Sheva pass the time. They spent the afternoon playing Monopoly, except that Sheva got up every fifteen minutes to look out the window.

"Are you going to put on your new coat to go down to the car, Sheva?"

"I sure am. I want Yehuda to see it as soon as he arrives."

"Good. The cleaners did a really neat job. You can't tell there was ever a chalk mark on it. Do Abie and Sammy ever talk to you or anything?"

"No, but then they hardly talk to anybody now. I think their parents really gave it to them. I know Rabbi Perloff meets with them every Friday because I've seen them in his office. I heard they help take care of Mr. Cohen. You know him, don't you?"

"He lives on Wightman Street. He's the man who lives alone and just had an operation, isn't he?"

"Yes. They're doing his shopping."

"Great! It's about time Sammy and Abie did something nice for a change. Listen, it's getting dark. I'd better get home before my mother starts to worry. Have a great time this Chanuka, Sheva."

"Thanks. I know I will. You too, Devora."

"Thanks. See you," called Devora as she ran down the stairs. Two seconds later, she came racing back up.

"They're here, Sheva. They're here!"

Her heart racing, Sheva grabbed her coat and went flying down the stairs and out the front door. She was so startled at what she saw that she had to sit down for a minute on the front step. There were three grinning boys in front of her. Not only had Yehuda come home, but Yitzy and Shlomo had come too!

As soon as Sheva caught her breath, she ran to her brothers, jumping up and down and hugging each one in turn. Mrs. Schwartz, hearing all the commotion, came to the door and was almost as excited as Sheva.

"Does Mama know?" asked Sheva.

"Yes, kitten," said Shlomo, "we called her Monday at the store to tell her, but we wanted to surprise you."

"No wonder she cooked and baked so much," said Sheva. "What a wonderful surprise!"

They were carrying the luggage from the car when Mrs. Markowitz got off the bus. She ran to her children and all the hugging and kissing started over again. Mrs. Schwartz was kept busy wiping her eyes with her handkerchief. It was so good to see the Markowitzes happy for a change. "Tch," she whispered under her breath, "too bad Mr. Markowitz couldn't be here, too."

Sheva was so excited that evening that she was giddy—laughing, talking, crying, hugging and laughing again. She hated to go to sleep that night. She hugged the boys as if they would disappear when they went downstairs to sleep in the Schwartzes' spare room. As Sheva lay awaked on the couch, the moon shone brightly through the attic window and she watched the stars.

"Oh, *Hashem*," she whispered, "even though I'm so happy and I thank you so much, I'm still not happy enough. I'm happy because my brothers are home, but I'm sad because my father is away. Please, please, *Hashem*, make my father get well. It's been so long since I've seen him."

Mrs. Markowitz also lay awake. She heard the softly whispered words of her daughter and smiled to herself. That night, she slept soundly.

Erev Shabbos, Mrs. Markowitz didn't go to work. Yehuda was going to borrow Tuvya's car and drive her to the convalescent home to see her husband. It was a visiting weekend. Sheva begged to come along each time Mrs. Markowitz went, but each time she received the same answer, "Children are not allowed. You know that, Sheva."

"Here, take Daddy this poem I wrote for him, and take this yarmulke I knitted him for Chanuka," said Sheva.

"Say, did you really make this yourself?" asked Yitzy.

"Very nice," said Shlomo.

"Can you make me one, too?" asked Yehuda.

"Of course I can. Do you really want one?" asked Sheva.

"We all do," said Shlomo.

Sheva was bursting with happiness.

"Now, boys, you and Sheva will have to get

everything ready for Shabbos Chanuka because it is quite a trip to the home and back."

"Don't worry, Mama, everything will be just fine," Sheva assured her.

Sheva and her two brothers entertained each other all day long. They talked and talked. Sheva felt that she had never talked so much in her whole life. With so much extra help, the house was soon ready for Shabbos. "Things go much faster when you have company and are happy," thought Sheva.

"You know what?" she asked suddenly. "I never told you how I got my new coat!"

She began telling them the long story of how she had found the glasses, searched for the owner and met Mrs. Goodman, and how Devora had gone back to speak to the elderly woman. Her brothers listened to every word. They were very happy for her.

"Come on, Sheva. It's beginning to snow. Do you want to go for a walk in the snow with your new coat?" asked Yitzy.

"Yes, let's all go," she answered.

The boys took their coats and started down the stairs, when they heard voices and footsteps coming up. And there on the stairs, with Mrs. Markowitz and Yehuda, stood their *father!* He stood there all bundled up in a coat and hat and scarf, and he was smiling a great, big wonderful smile.

"Daddy, Daddy . . ." whispered Sheva.

"Dad, oh, Dad . . . you look great!" said Yitzy.

"Dad, you're home at last," murmered Shlomo.

"Daddy, Daddy, Daddy, it's really you! Oh, it's

really you," sobbed Sheva as she jumped up and threw her arms around her father's neck.

"Yes, *kinderlach. Baruch Hashem*, I'm home for good!" He hugged each of his children tightly, tears glistening in his eyes.

The family made their way back to the attic apartment. Though it had seemed small and crowded before, now it was big and wonderful, and once the Chanuka candles were lit, it was full of light and joy. Everyone talked and laughed and cried.

Mr. Markowitz told his children that the doctors said he was well enough to start working part-time, and that arrangements had already been made for him to substitute for Mrs. Stein, a teacher who was going on maternity leave. Mrs. Markowitz put money into the large charity boxes by the kitchen window, thanking *Hashem* that her husband was home and her family was whole and together again. Then she went to light the Shabbos candles.

The boys went off to *shul*, but the doctor had told Mr. Markowitz to rest after the long trip, so he *davened* at home. He sat on the couch while Sheva talked nonstop, retelling the story of her new coat.

"It's beautiful, Shevala. A perfect, blue plush coat. I'm so happy you have it. And I'm so happy to have *you*! I've missed you all so much. Your letters and poems were a great help to me when I was sick."

"I'm glad, Daddy," said Sheva, glowing with happiness.

When the boys came home from *shul*, they gathered around the kitchen table, all of them together for the first time in over two years. They waited with shining faces to hear their father make *kiddush*.

"*Kinderlach*, this is our Chanuka present—Daddy is home!" said Mrs. Markowitz. "Now, with God's help, everything is going to be all right."

"Yes," thought Elisheva. "Now that we are a family again, *baruch Hashem*, everything is going to be all right. This is the best Chanuka I've ever had—a perfect, blue plush Chanuka!"

❋ *Just This Once*

❋ Rena walked along the marble floor, her high heels clicking as she hurried to finish her last errand before closing time. It had been an exhausting day, and she was anxious to get home. Her footsteps resounded throughout the dim interior of the museum as she made her way through the Greek statuary and proceeded into the dinosaur room, the art gallery, past the animal exhibit, into the aquarium, and finally to the stairs that went down to the photostat department.

"I must walk a hundred miles a day," she thought to herself.

This was Rena's first job. She worked in the patent room of the main library in Baltimore, where she spent most of her time on the second floor, poring over heavy volumes of patent records. Occasionally she was sent to the photostat department with the cumbersome patent books to make copies of certain pages. At this moment she was on just such an errand. Glancing at her watch, she realized it was 4:50 PM—ten minutes until closing time.

"It's going to take me almost ten minutes just to walk there, and then I have to come all the way back," she thought. "I'll miss my bus."

A strand of her dark, curly hair fell over her forehead and into her eyes. Rena put down the big book she was carrying. As she gathered up her curls and pinned them into place, she realized that she was standing in front of the building's back elevator. Bits of overheard conversations raced through her mind.

"Don't use the old elevator. It gets stuck sometimes."

"Oh, it's all right. I use it all the time and nothing has ever happened."

"Well, old lady Nelson, the supervisor, said not to use it."

"Well, I do. I'm not going to walk all the way down to the photostat room ten times a day. Nothing will happen."

"Nothing will happen . . . nothing will happen . . . ," she thought over and over again as she debated whether or not to use the elevator and finish her errand in half the time so that she could catch her bus.

"Oh, nothing will happen, just this once," she said aloud and pressed the button.

Slowly but surely the elevator came up the shaft. It ground to a halt and the door creaked open. Lifting the heavy patent volume, Rena gingerly entered the old-fashioned cage and seated herself on the round seat in the corner. Resting the heavy book on her lap, she pressed the lowest green button, and the heavy door slid shut. A violent lurch almost knocked her from the seat as the elevator began to groan loudly and descend to the basement.

"Well, at least it's moving," said Rena. "Oh, I spoke too soon!" The elevator had stopped.

She waited patiently as she recalled another bit of overheard conversation: "It stops and starts a lot. Sometimes I think the stairs are faster than that elevator." Rena waited and waited for the feeling of movement, but there was none.

"Oh, boy," she sighed, pushing the little green button again and again. But nothing happened. She tried the second green button and waited . . . but again, nothing happened. She tried the last button . . . but nothing happened then either.

"O.K., I'll press the emergency button," she said to herself. She searched the elevator carefully, but there was no emergency button.

"Well, then, I guess I'll have to call for help."

"Help! Help! Somebody help! I'm stuck in the elevator. Help!" screamed Rena at the top of her lungs, hoping her voice would penetrate the heavy door.

She continued to shout, when she suddenly realized that no one would hear her cries for help because everyone had probably left the building already. A look at her watch confirmed her fears. It was 5:02 PM.

"Oh, my," gulped Rena, as a queer sinking sensation filled her stomach, "I'm stuck in this elevator, in an empty building, all alone, and no one even knows I'm here."

For the first time, she panicked. She trembled

slightly and her knees buckled. Her heart started pounding so quickly that it felt as if it would fly out of her chest. It kept racing on . . . harder and faster, until she was panting for breath. Beads of perspiration covered her face.

"I might die," she thought to herself. "I might die and no one would even know I'm here." Rena saw black spots before her eyes. Then there was darkness.

When she regained consciousness, Rena wasn't quite sure what had happened. She didn't remember fainting, but she found herself lying on the floor of the elevator, dizzy but calmer. Soon she felt well enough to sit up and assess the situation. She made a mental list:

1. There was no point in yelling for help.

2. The elevator transom was open so there was enough oxygen.

3. She was hungry, but she did have several pieces of hard candy in her skirt pocket to quiet her rumbling stomach.

4. Her parents would surely alert the police when she failed to arrive home.

"My parents," she thought to herself, "my poor parents . . . They'll be so worried about me. Oy! I hate to cause them any kind of pain. I know they'll just be frantic! Oh, *Hashem*, let me get out of here *soon* so that my parents won't worry!"

Then she took a deep breath and continued her mental list:

5. Don't take chances like this again — ever!! A Jew is not allowed to put himself in danger.

6. Maybe maintenance people will come to work and she could make enough noise to be heard by them.

7. Study the elevator. Maybe there is a possibility of a way out.

Rena took one of the candies out of her skirt pocket, unwrapped it, made a *bracha* and popped it into her mouth. She tried to relax and enjoy the sweet, peppermint taste for a few moments, and then she got up from the floor.

She pushed the buttons again, one at a time, two at a time . . . all three together, but with no results. The elevator didn't move. She sat down on the round seat and began to pray aloud.

"Please, *Hashem,* my parents are going to worry terribly. They won't know what happened to me, and they'll imagine all kinds of awful things. Please don't let them be too upset. Let me think of a way to get out of here before it gets dark. It's a good thing it's summer and the days are longer.

"Why did this happen to me anyway? Nothing happens by coincidence or chance. Did I do something wrong? I hope not, but if I did, I'm truly sorry. If I could only think of what I might have done, I would try and do proper *teshuva* for it! Oh, please, *Hashem,* help me out of here!"

Rena tried all the buttons again, but nothing happened. A tear trickled out of the corner of her eye and was quickly wiped away.

"Cut it out, Rena," she said, mentally shaking herself. "Crying doesn't help. And, anyway, *Hashem* knows what's happening and He's in control, so stop it right now!"

She sat staring at the walls until she suddenly had an idea. She removed one of her shoes and stuck the thin heel into the space between the elevator doors. Maybe she could force the door open and climb out. She pushed and shoved until her face was red and her arm sore. She pushed so hard that she did manage to make a small opening, but it did not make her happy. What she saw was a solid cement wall. The elevator was stuck between floors!

She was overcome by a feeling of hopelessness. "Who knows if I'll *ever* get out of here. No one uses the elevator much. No one knows I'm here. Everyone is gone. If I've learned anything from all this, it's that a person is not allowed to put himself in a dangerous situation, which is exactly what I did. My parents must be frantic by now. Maybe they're calling the police. But even if they do, they won't think of looking for me here. Oh, *Hashem,* please help me. Get me out of here!" She sobbed quietly.

Time dragged on. It seemed like hours. Rena was getting very hungry. Her last meal had been at 11:30 that morning. She took another candy from her pocket, but it only whet her appetite.

She cried off and on and prayed harder than she had ever prayed before. Finally, her eyes filled with tears, Rena leaned back against the elevator wall. Suddenly, she heard a loud, grating noise, and a violent jolt threw her forward to the floor. Miracle of miracles, Rena felt the elevator rise!

"It's supposed to be going down," she thought, "but what's the difference—it's moving! It's moving!"

And move it did—right back up to where it had started from. The moment it stopped and the door opened, Rena grabbed the patent volume and ran out to glorious freedom. She ran all the way back to the first floor front desk to call her parents. She must be hours late.

"Hello . . . Ma? I'm OK. Really. I'm just fine, so don't worry."

"Worry?" answered her mother. "Why should I worry? Is something wrong?"

Rena was puzzled. "Because I'm so late," she said.

"Late? You're usually not home until 6."

Rena glanced down at her watch. It was only 5:25!

❋ *What Happened to Milly?*

❋ Milly lived around the corner from me in the big white house on Brentley Street. It had a porch that stretched from one end of the house to the other. When Milly's mother wasn't home, we loved to skate back and forth on the porch, and every time we reached one spot in the corner, it went "bloop blap bloop blap."

Milly was lots of fun. We did crazy things together. We used to take these long walks. At every corner we'd flip a penny to decide in which direction to go. Sometimes we'd end up walking around the same block six times and sometimes we'd end up on Fifth Avenue. That was the part we liked best. Behind a stone wall on Fifth Avenue was a vine-covered house with a smashed window in the attic and bars on the downstairs windows. The stories we imagined about that place would make your hair stand on end. Sometimes we scared ourselves so much that we stayed away from there for weeks.

Milly and I became best friends, and every Shabbos

after we ate, I'd run over to her house. At first my parents didn't say anything, but one Shabbos, my father called me into his study.

"Yehudis, come here. I want to speak to you."

"Yes, Daddy, what is it?"

"I see you really like this girl, Milly."

"She's my best friend."

"If she is such a good friend, why doesn't she ever come here on Shabbos? Why do you always go there?"

"I think it's because we keep Shabbos."

"What does that mean, Yehudis?"

"Well, since they don't keep Shabbos, her mother doesn't want her to come here."

"Why not?"

"I don't know. Maybe she thinks Milly will bother us or something."

"I see. Are they afraid that perhaps Milly might like Shabbos here?"

"I don't know."

"Do you think it is proper for *you* to spend a good part of every Shabbos in a house that does *not* keep Shabbos?"

"But *I* keep it, Daddy. I don't do anything I shouldn't. You know that."

"I know, Yehudis. But still, I repeat, do you think you should spend such a large part of every Shabbos in a house that does not keep the Shabbos?"

I sat there, looking at my father's clear blue eyes as he spoke to me. Even though I was child, I detected the tinge of disappointment. I looked at his black Shabbos suit, the one with the vest. It was my favorite. I must have looked at it for a long time because he asked me again: "Well . . . do you?"

"I don't know," I answered.

"Don't you?"

"But, Daddy, I ask her to come here, but she doesn't come."

"I am truly sorry about that, but, Yehudis, I am afraid that perhaps you are losing some of the *kedusha*, the holiness of Shabbos, by spending so much time at Milly's house each week."

I didn't go to Milly's house that Shabbos, nor the next, nor the next. In fact I didn't go to Milly's house at all, and she didn't come to mine either.

About a month later, I was walking home from *shul* with my family, and as we crossed Morely Avenue, Milly darted from her porch towards us. She ran up to me, grabbed me and whispered into my ear, "I'll be at your house at two o'clock." Then she raced back, her hair flying in the wind, and slammed the door shut behind her. We all looked at each other. Nobody said anything as we went home to make *kiddush* and eat.

All through the meal my heart was beating with anticipation and excitement. Ever since all this had started, I hadn't been able to face Milly, because I knew my father was right. But how could I explain it to Milly who didn't understand these things? I thought she would think I didn't want to be best friends any more. Then, when she didn't come to see me, I thought she was mad at *me*. Now maybe we could be friends again. I had really missed her.

At two o'clock sharp there was a knock at the kitchen door. I ran to answer it and there was Milly, all dressed up, standing shyly at the entrance. We both stood there awkwardly for a minute.

"Hi," I finally said.

She grabbed me and smiled and hugged me hard. "Oh, I've missed you."

"Me, too," I answered, and everything was all right again.

We went to my room and sat cross-legged on the ruffled pink bedspreads, each of us holding pillows in our laps.

"How come you're all dressed up, Milly?"

"Because it's Shabbos in your house."

"Oh. That's nice of you. How come your parents let you come?"

"Gee, I missed you so much, Judy. They knew how miserable I was, so they said I could come."

"I'm glad. Are we still best friends?"

"Best friends — you bet."

We stayed in my bedroom for about two hours before Milly would go into the front room. When we finally got there, she saw my father learning *gemara* and she asked me what he was doing. I explained that he was learning Torah.

"Why does he do it out loud?" she asked.

"Because if you hear the words, it helps you understand and remember it better."

Later, when she got a closer look at the *gemara*, she asked, "Is that what Hebrew looks like? How can you read that?"

I was shocked. Milly had never even seen Hebrew letters! I suddenly realized how little she knew about being Jewish.

"You mean, you can't read Hebrew?" I exclaimed.

"Uh huh. I never went to Sunday school or anything. Is it hard to learn?"

"No, not at all. Kindergarten kids learn to read."

"Come on," said Milly, changing the subject, "let's go for a walk."

I looked over to my father for his approval, and he smiled and nodded. I led Milly through the kitchen and stopped short at the plate of chocolate chip cookies my mother had put out.

"Give Milly some cookies and soda," said my mother with a smile. "There, sit down, girls, I'll get some glasses."

I took a cookie and made the *bracha*. "What are you saying?" asked Milly.

"It's a blessing to God for having given us this food. We say blessings before and after everything we eat."

"Oh. Should I do it, too?"

"Sure, I'll help you. Just say it after me."

We finished eating and went for a walk. We walked all the way to Frick Park. I used to enjoy walking through the park and sitting on the benches near the wading pool. Sometimes we'd walk over the trails, but I wasn't allowed to do that without a grownup, so now we just sat on the grass and talked. After a while, I told Milly I had to get home for *seuda shelishis*.

"What's that?" she asked.

"It's the third Shabbos meal."

"What do you do?"

"Well, some boys who are my brother's age come to learn with my father every Shabbos. They usually stay and eat with us. But this week, my mother's Sunday school class is coming, too. We'll have a nice time. Want to come? My parents won't mind."

"I don't know. Maybe my parents wouldn't want me to."

"Ask them. Go ahead, please."

"Look, let's go. You go home. If I can come, I'll be right over. OK? If not, don't be mad."

"I won't."

"Promise?"

"Promise."

We were all pleasantly surprised that Milly came.

There were about twenty kids in our house that Shabbos. My father learned *Pirkey Avos*—Ethics of the Fathers. Then everyone sang the Shabbos *zemiros*, and my father told stories, just like he always does. My father tells wonderful stories. After that, we ate. My mother made delicious macaroni salad and deviled eggs, and we had ice cream for dessert. Everyone had a great time, especially Milly. She leaned over during dessert and whispered, "Do you do this every Shabbos?"

"Pretty often," I said.

"Boy, you have fun," she said with a bit of envy in her voice.

As the weeks passed Milly used to pop in on Shabbos from time to time. By the next summer, she was a regular Shabbos guest.

That year we both graduated from sixth grade. She graduated from public school and I graduated from Hebrew Academy. Milly was all set to go to Alderson High when the busing laws were passed. I didn't have a problem—I would go to junior high school at Hebrew Academy, but Milly and her parents were in a dilemma. She was notified that she would be bused to a school on the other side of town. I suggested to Milly that she come to Hebrew Academy with me, but her parents wouldn't hear of it. Private schools were opening up all over because so many parents opposed busing their children across town. Milly's mother and father sent for applications to all of them.

For weeks Milly was taking one test after another to get into these schools. Her parents bragged that she would get into the best school there was. Milly was smart. They had had her tested and her IQ was 138 (that's almost genius!).

One afternoon in the middle of July, Milly came over to see me. She looked very unhappy.

"What's the matter Milly?"

"Can you believe it? I failed every entrance exam I took! I can't understand it. Me, Milly—I failed! Don't think I'm snobby, Judy, but you know what I mean."

I knew what she meant. Milly was known as a brain. She always got A's and received all kinds of awards.

"I can't understand how *you* could fail. Are you sure? Maybe there's some mistake?"

"No mistake. I failed."

"Could you take the tests over or something?"

"I did already, Judy. Can you believe it? I failed

them all *twice!* I just don't understand it. Some kids who make C's all the time got in, but not me."

Milly's parents hired a tutor. She had only one more chance. If she didn't make it by the third try, she'd have to wait until next year. I didn't see Milly at all for a while. She was always busy studying. Then one hot afternoon in August, Milly appeared at our kitchen door.

"Hi, Milly! How are you? What's happening with your tests?"

"I failed again," she said with a grimace. "My parents are so upset. Actually, upset is not the word for it! I guess I'll have to be bused. That means getting up at 6 o'clock, getting home at 5. And who wants to go to school miles from home?"

That evening at supper, I told my parents what had happened. My father said maybe he should get Rabbi Bergman to talk to Milly's parents. My mother thought it was a good idea.

And guess what? As a result of their conversation, Milly enrolled at Hebrew Academy! Was I glad! My mother had Milly over to the house every day to give her private lessons in reading Hebrew. She learned in less than a month. I never understood how she could learn something new so fast and so well, and yet fail the tests on everything she had already learned before.

Milly loved Hebrew Academy. She absorbed everything that was taught, and before the year was up, she was begging her parents to *kasher* their kitchen. She learned to speak Hebrew fairly well during her first year, and she made excellent grades. In the spring, her parents wanted her tested for a private school again. Milly wasn't at all happy about this, but she complied with their wishes. Would you believe that she failed again? I was beginning to think she did it on purpose, but she swore up and down that she really tried to pass, because things at home were getting difficult for her. Her father was sure that she had some psychological problem, and he was determined to discover what it was.

In our sophomore year, my family moved to New York, but Milly and I kept in touch. She ended up graduating from Hebrew Academy, but after graduation, we sort of lost track of each other until three years later when she invited me to her wedding. I was delighted. She was marrying Sol Katzen. I remembered Sol from Hebrew Academy very well. "That's really terrific!" I thought to myself. "They'll keep Shabbos and kosher and everything!"

After that we sent each other New Year cards every Rosh Hashana. Just recently I received a letter from her, the first real letter in many years. It said:

Dear Judy and Label,

I just wanted to let you know that our oldest son Simcha just received his *semicha*. You don't know how proud and happy I am. Even my parents are thrilled. I bet they never thought they'd have a rabbi in the family!

As I sit and think about the events in years past, my thoughts often drift to those years in Junior High when I failed all my exams to private schools. At the time, I couldn't understand it. Now I know I was destined to fail, and I am thankful to *Hashem* for having guided me along paths which led to a life of meaning and happiness. I thank Him, too, for having given me a friend like you who helped show me the way. You and your family have a share in every *mitzva* I perform.

May *Hashem* bless you and yours with *bracha* and *hatzlacha* always.

With sincere affection,
Malka (Milly)